FOREST

OF THE

SASQUATCH

THEIR TERRITORY, THEIR RULES

LUKA T. JACOBS

Cover Design, Book Design & Formatting: Luka T. Jacobs.

To my Dad: I'd choose you in every lifetime.

NOTE FROM THE AUTHOR

Thank you for embarking on this wild and chilling journey into the *Forest of the Sasquatch*. Writing this story has been a thrilling adventure, and knowing it's now in your hands fills me with deep gratitude.

To those who crave tales of survival, suspense, and the untamed unknown—this book was crafted with you in mind. I hope it will keep you on the edge of your seat and ignite your imagination and sense of wonder.

If you enjoy this adventure, I'd love to hear from you! Reviews, messages, and word-of-mouth recommendations mean the world to indie authors like me.

Thank you again for stepping into the forest with me.

Luka T. Jacobs

FB: https://www.facebook.com/lukatjacobs
A: https://amazon.com/author/lukatjacobs
W: http://www.LukaTJacobs.com

CONTENTS

PROLOGUE

The forest breathed its ancient rhythm. High above, the towering pines swayed in the autumn breeze, their needles whispering secrets carried through ancient shadows. Sunlight filtered through the dense canopy, dappling the forest floor in patches of amber and gold.

Hidden deep within the Superior National Forest, near Devil's Track Lake, where the trees cast the deepest shadows, lay a place untouched by humans–the clan's secret sanctuary.

Even the animals of the forest seemed to sense the boundary of this sacred ground, avoiding it entirely. Deer grazed near its edges but never crossed into its heart. Birds flew above the cliffs but rarely landed near the cave's entrance. The natural world seemed to understand what the hairless ones could not: this place belonged to the Sasquatch alone.

Thick, unyielding walls of thorny thicket and dense brush surrounded the area, growing so tightly together that even the smallest creatures struggled to pass through. Towering trees formed a natural barrier, their twisted roots and low-hanging branches weaving into an almost impenetrable maze. Beyond the thicket, a sheer cliff face rose abruptly from the earth, its jagged surface streaked with moss and lichen. At its base, hidden among boulders and shadows, was the entrance to a vast cave system, cool and damp, where the clan had lived for generations.

The caves were a place of safety, a haven where the family slept, gathered, and raised their young. Here, in this untouched wilderness, the Sasquatch thrived, living in harmony with the forest. But their peace was fragile. The hairless ones had grown bold, venturing deeper into the forest, leaving trails of destruction in their wake.

Aluk crouched low beneath the brush, his eyes glinting as he watched a pair of hairless ones far below. He and his brother Matto had left the sanctuary to patrol the edges of their territory, as they often did when the hairless ones grew too bold. What they saw now made Aluk's fists clench.

The two hairless ones had arrived in a roaring metal

beast, its tires gouging deep ruts into the soft earth. They had parked it at the edge of a clearing, its bulk looming like an unwelcome guest. One of them—a tall hairless one in a bright orange jacket—was crouched over the lifeless body of a deer, its glossy eyes staring blankly into the dirt. The hairless one's hands were red with blood as he hacked at the carcass with a hunting knife, his movements rough and careless.

The second hairless one, stocky with a scruffy beard, stood nearby, gathering sticks. "Told you this spot was good," he said, his voice carrying across the clearing. "Nobody comes out this far."

"Think they'll notice one less deer?" the tall hairless one asked, his laugh sharp and grating.

Aluk growled softly, his breath steaming in the cool evening air. His eyes darted to the thunder stick lying in the dirt near the stocky one's feet. A weapon capable of death from a distance—one the clan had learned to fear.

The deer was theirs. The clan depended on these woods for food. The hairless ones had not only invaded their sacred ground—they had stolen from it.

Matto placed a hand on Aluk's shoulder, his claws brushing against the coarse hair there. Through gestures and images, Matto conveyed his thoughts: *Hold. Wait. The Elder forbids this.*

Aluk's response came in a flood of sharp, vivid images: the hairless ones' bloody hands, their trash scattering across the sacred ground, the machine scarring the earth. *They destroy. They take. How much longer will we watch?*

Matto hesitated. He shared Aluk's anger, but the Elder's warning rang in his mind. The Elder had long insisted on secrecy, on patience. But patience had not stopped the hairless ones from encroaching farther each year.

Hidden in the tree line, Aluk, and Matto crouched, watching as the hairless ones built their red-breath. The breath licked high into the sky, casting flickering shadows on the trees. One of the hairless ones stood and stretched, letting out a loud belch.

"I'm gonna take a piss," he said, stumbling toward the forest's edge.

The men wrinkled their noses as an awful stench wafted toward them. It was rank and overpowering, like garbage left out in the sun for days, layered with a heavy musk that clung to the back of their throats.

"Geez, what is that smell?" one of them mumbled, turning his head away.

Aluk's massive body tensed. He glanced at Matto, who raised a hand in warning. The elder's unspoken message was clear: *hold back. Watch, but do not act.*

But Aluk's mind surged with defiance. He sent an image of the hairless ones laughing, their red-breath consuming the sacred ground, the machine scarring the earth. *Enough.*

As the hairless one staggered toward the trees, Aluk shifted silently from his vantage point, slipping through the thick underbrush. His movements were precise, his hulking frame ghostlike in the moonlight as he circled closer. The rustle of the leaves, the crack of twigs—sounds that would have betrayed a human—blended seamlessly with the forest's natural rhythm.

The hairless one stopped a few feet from the tree line, fumbling with his belt. Aluk waited, crouched just beyond the brush, his eyes locked on his target.

Before Matto could stop him, Aluk lunged forward.

The hairless one barely had time to gasp before Aluk's hand clamped over his face, silencing him. In one swift motion, Aluk dragged the hairless one into the thickets. There was a muffled cry, then silence.

Back at the red-breath, the second hairless one looked up, frowning. "Derek?" he called, squinting into the darkness.

"Quit screwing around, man."

He heard something—a faint rustling from the direction Derek had gone. Then, the snapping of branches. A silhouette moved at the edge of the firelight, massive and looming, too large to be anything human.

A wave of panic washed over him, accompanied by a deep, unsettling fear. He stumbled back toward the clearing, nearly tripping over his own feet. His eyes darted around, trying to pierce the blackness. "Derek?" he called again, his voice trembling now.

When no response came, he turned and sprinted toward his four-wheeler parked near the fire. His hands fumbled as he started the machine, the engine roaring to life. The noise echoed through the forest, jarring and unnatural.

"Not sticking around for this crap," he mumbled, his voice shaking as he gripped the handlebars and gunned the throttle. The four-wheeler lurched forward, kicking up dirt and leaves as it sped down the narrow trail towards the clearing's edge.

The trail was dark, lit only by the pale beams of the machine's headlight. The hairless one's pulse quickened, the trees seeming to converge, their shadows alive with an unseen, unsettling presence. He glanced over his shoulder, expecting to see something chasing him.

As he glanced back at the trail, his eyes widened in disbelief.

Standing in the middle of the path was a towering figure, its hair gleaming faintly in the four-wheeler's headlights. The creature's glowing amber eyes locked on him, and its massive form blocked the trail entirely.

"Jesus Christ!" the hairless one screamed, shifting his weight as he jerked the handlebars in a frantic attempt to avoid the creature.

The four-wheeler skidded out of control, its tires losing traction on the dirt. The hairless one's panic made him overcompensate, and the machine careened off the trail. It slammed headfirst into a tree with a sickening crunch, the force throwing the hairless one forward.

His body hit the tree with brutal force, a sharp thud reverberating in the woods. He crumpled to the ground at its base, groaning in pain. Blood poured from a deep gash on his forehead as he tried to crawl away, but his body betrayed him, too stunned to respond.

Aluk and Matto emerged silently from the darkness.

The brothers towered over the injured hairless one and

the machine that had defiled their sacred forest. Aluk's lips curled back in a snarl as he sent an image to Matto: the machine broken, destroyed, its noise silenced forever.

Matto stepped forward first, his massive hands gripping the four-wheeler. With a guttural roar, he lifted the machine as though it weighed nothing and slammed it into the ground. Metal crumpled and shattered under the force.

The hairless one whimpered, struggling to drag himself away. His effort was futile.

Aluk advanced, his amber eyes cold. His massive hand reached down, cutting off the hairless one's final, strangled scream.

When the forest fell silent once more, the brothers walked back toward the clearing.

The red-breath still burned faintly, casting flickering light across the remains of the deer carcass the hairless ones had stolen from the woods. Aluk crouched beside it, running his massive hands over the animal's body. Its spirit belonged to the forest, not to the hairless ones who had taken it without care or honor.

With a series of deliberate gestures and vivid shared images, Aluk and Matto came to an agreement: the deer would not be left here to rot. Nor would the bodies of the hairless ones remain to poison the sacred ground.

Matto hoisted the deer across his shoulder with ease, its lifeless form dangling against his broad back. His gaze lingered on the thunder stick lying in the dirt, its metal surface gleaming faintly. With a deliberate motion, he bent down, picked it up, and secured it alongside the deer. He had no idea what he was going to do with the weapon, but he knew he couldn't leave it behind for other hairless ones to find and use.

Aluk carried the bodies of the two hairless ones, their weight inconsequential against his immense strength. The brothers cast a final glance at the campsite—and disappeared into the forest.

****

As the first light of dawn painted the horizon, the brothers returned to the sanctuary. Matto laid the deer at the center of the main cave, where it would be divided among the clan. Aluk turned to face the Elder, his chest heaving with the weight of his anger and pride.

The Elder's amber eyes flicked from the bloodied brothers to the deer and back again. Aluk's shared images depicted the events: the hairless ones stealing what was not theirs, the loud machine ravaging the land, and the brothers' swift retribution.

The Elder's expression remained unreadable, but his thoughts were firm. *You have acted without permission. You risked exposure.*

Aluk's response came quickly, sharp and unrelenting: We protected the forest. The hairless ones are no longer. The deer is ours again.

Matto added his agreement, showing an image of the clan gathered around the deer, nourished by what had been stolen. *This is our duty. To guard. To provide.*

The Elder stared at them for a long moment before turning toward the depths of the cave. His final thought was projected to the whole clan: *You have risked more than you know. But tonight, the forest has been restored.*

CHAPTER 1

The bar smelled like cheap beer and fried food. Dim lighting filtered through a haze of chatter and cigarette smoke from the back patio, where a small crowd lingered despite the cool October air. Televisions mounted above the bar played a football game, the commentator's voice barely audible over the hum of conversation.

Levi pushed the door open and stepped inside, shaking off the evening chill.

He scanned the room until his eyes landed on Carter, already at their usual spot in the corner. The guy was easy to spot—tall and lean, with a perpetual slouch that made him seem more laid-back than he really was. His slightly messy dark hair and the faint hint of a 5-o'clock shadow added to his scruffy, unpolished charm. He was throwing back a beer while scrolling through his phone, his sharp, blue eyes flicking across the screen.

Levi crossed the room, dodging a waitress balancing a tray of wings, and slid onto the stool next to him.

Carter didn't look up. "Took you long enough."

"Had to stop by Abby's first," Levi said, shrugging out of his jacket. He motioned to the bartender. "Just a beer."

"She kick you out for the night?" Carter asked, a smirk tugging at the corners of his mouth.

Levi rolled his eyes. "Hardly. She told me to remind you not to forget your tent this weekend. Apparently, she still remembers the time you spent the entire night swatting mosquitoes because you 'didn't think it would rain.'"

Carter chuckled softly. "That was one time."

"And yet she brings it up every year," Levi said with a grin.

The bartender slid a bottle across the counter, and Levi took a sip before leaning back in his seat. "You good?"

Carter shrugged. "Yeah. Long day at work, but it's whatever. You?"

"Same old," Levi said. "Dad's got me on a cabin remodel over by Birch Lake. Guy wants it done before winter hits, so we're scrambling."

Carter nodded, his gaze drifting to the TV screen.

A faint clink of glass sounded nearby, drawing their attention briefly. Before Levi could turn back, a tipsy blonde approached their corner. She wobbled slightly as she leaned on the bar, her smile wide and bold as she locked eyes with Levi.

"Hey, cutie," she said, her words slurring just enough to make it clear she'd had more than a few drinks. She reached out, placing her hand lightly on Levi's arm. "Wanna play a round of pool with me?"

Levi glanced at her hand, then back at her face. He offered a polite smile and shook his head. "Thanks, but I'm good. Just here to catch up with my buddy."

She pouted, swaying slightly on her feet, but eventually shrugged and wandered off toward the pool tables.

Carter was grinning before she was even out of earshot. He turned to Levi, shaking his head. "Does that kind of shit happen every time you go out? Or is it just the Brad Pitt thing you've got going on?"

Levi raised an eyebrow. "What are you talking about?"

"You know exactly what I'm talking about," Carter said, gesturing vaguely at him. "The blonde sandy hair, the blue eyes, the tall, athletic frame—like, seriously, man. It's ridiculous."

Levi snorted. "No, that does not happen every time. And I don't know what kind of fantasy world you're living in, but I'm no Brad Pitt."

"Yeah, sure," Carter said, rolling his eyes. "Keep pretending."

Levi shook his head, chuckling softly, and turned back to his beer.

The conversation shifted as the bartender brought them fresh drinks, and they both settled in, talking about the weekend's camping trip.

Carter's phone buzzed on the bar, lighting up briefly. He glanced at it, smirking.

"Rob?" Levi asked, already guessing.

"Yeah," Carter said, shaking his head. "He's not coming. Says he's 'caught up in wedding prep.'" He made air quotes with one hand while picking up his beer with the other.

Levi laughed. "Wedding prep? What's Bree got him doing now—folding napkins?"

"Wouldn't be the first time," Carter said. "Remember when she roped him into that candle-making thing last year?"

Levi snorted. "Oh, I remember. He was covered in wax for a week. Said it was 'therapeutic.'"

Carter shook his head, his grin widening. "Anyway, he says we'll have to survive without him tonight. Typical Rob—can't even show up for a beer."

"He'll make up for it this weekend," Levi said. "Bet he's already packed a cooler full of craft beer."

"The '#1 Party Starter,'" Carter said, rolling his eyes.

"Guaranteed," Levi said, grinning.

"You packed for the trip?" Levi asked after a moment.

"Yeah, most of it," Carter said. "Borrowed a few things from my dad. Should be good."

"You don't sound excited."

Carter shrugged. "Camping's not really my thing, you know that. But it's Rob's bucks party, so I'll deal."

"Hey, at least it's not one of those big, ridiculous parties with strippers and limo rides," Levi said.

"True," Carter said, a faint smile tugging at his lips. "It should be a fun, relaxing weekend."

"Not unless Tyson pulls a stunt," Levi said, grinning.

Carter chuckled. "The twins are coming?"

"Yep," Levi said. "Tyson and Tyler. They're driving up from Minneapolis tomorrow."

"Haven't seen them in years," Carter said, shaking his head. "Tyson's probably still cracking dumb jokes, isn't he?"

"Like he never stopped," Levi said. "And Tyler? He's still the guy questioning everything. 'You sure that trail leads somewhere? You sure that's not poison ivy?' He'll probably have us second-guessing every step of the way."

Carter laughed softly. "Good crew, though."

"Yeah," Levi said. "Should be fun."

They both turned their attention to the game on the TV above the bar. The Vikings were scrambling to keep their lead, and Levi leaned forward slightly, his beer bottle resting loosely in his hands.

"Think they'll hold on?" Levi asked.

"Not with that defense," Carter replied, his eyes narrowing as the quarterback barely escaped a sack.

The nearby table erupted in cheers as the Vikings eked out a first down. Levi glanced sideways at Carter, noticing the way he kept fiddling with his phone, flipping it face-down every time it lit up.

"You sure you're good?" Levi asked.

Carter hesitated, then nodded. "Yeah. Just some work crap."

Levi raised an eyebrow. "Work crap doesn't usually have you glued to your phone."

Carter sighed. "It's nothing. Really."

Levi didn't press further, but he wasn't convinced.

"Well, forget about it for the weekend," Levi said. "No cell service out there, remember? Just us, the woods, and the campfire."

Carter chuckled softly, though his expression remained distant. "Sounds peaceful."

"It will be," Levi said.

By the time they stepped outside, the air had grown colder, biting against their faces as they lingered near the bar's entrance. White Bear Lake's streets lay hushed, illuminated only by the faint glow of streetlights.

"You heading home?" Carter asked, shoving his hands into his jacket pockets.

"Yeah," Levi said. "I need my beauty sleep."

"Right," Carter chuckled.

"You heading out too?" Levi queried.

"Nah, might stick around for another beer," Carter said, his tone casual.

"All right. Just don't show up hungover tomorrow," Levi said, clapping him on the shoulder.

Carter laughed lightly. "No promises."

As Levi walked to his truck, he glanced back. Carter stood in the same spot, a cigarette glowing faintly between his fingers as he stared into the distance, his expression unreadable. Levi hesitated, debating whether to say something, but then slid into the driver's seat. Whatever was weighing on Carter's mind would have to wait.

Behind him, the neon sign of the bar buzzed faintly in the

cold night air. Carter took a final drag, exhaled slowly, and flicked the cigarette away before turning and heading back inside.

CHAPTER 2

The forest around Devil's Track Lake lay in hushed stillness, broken only by the soft rustle of leaves stirred by the cool night breeze. Moonlight filtered through the towering trees, casting faint patterns on the ground.

After feasting on the reclaimed deer, the clan rested in their cave, their growls and murmurs echoing softly through the sacred space. Outside, the night carried on, undisturbed, as if the forest itself acknowledged their dominance.

Near the mouth of the main cave, Aluk stood rigid, his eyes fixed on the Elder, who sat on a flat stone within the darkness. Matto shifted beside him, his heavy frame taut with anticipation.

The Elder's disapproval hung heavy in the air. Flashes of memory flickered between them—the blood-streaked clearing, the shattered remains of the hairless ones' machine, and the broken balance the brothers had caused.

"*You acted rashly,*" the Elder's thoughts growled, paired with a low rumble from his chest. "*You risked everything.*"

Aluk's muscles tensed, his teeth clenched as he responded with sharp, vivid images: the roaring machine tearing up the earth, the lifeless deer stolen from the sanctuary, the red-breath consuming sacred ground. His grunt was sharp, defiant.

"They came into our sanctuary," his thoughts snarled, vivid with memory. "*They took what is ours. We protected it.*"

Matto stepped forward, his own grunt low and resonant, adding weight to his brother's defiance. "*If we do nothing, they will return. They will take more. They must learn this land is not theirs. We are tired of watching and doing nothing.*"

The Elder remained still, his thoughts measured but unyielding. "*If you strike, more will come. They will bring red-breath and thunder-sticks.*"

A low growl rumbled from Aluk's chest, frustration rolling off him like a storm. His thought-images flared again: hairless ones fleeing in terror, their machines destroyed, the forest restored. *"Then we destroy them too. But we will not let them take more. We will only act if they come near. This is not war—it is defense."*

Aluk turned sharply from the Elder, his massive shoulders squared. Matto followed as they strode toward the clearing where the clan had begun to gather, their hulking forms blending with the darkness.

When Aluk reached the group, he raised his arms and released a low, resonant grunt that commanded attention. The group stirred, their eyes catching the pale glow of the moonlight.

A deep snarl rumbled from Aluk's chest as he projected a sequence of memories into the minds of the gathered Sasquatch: hairless ones cutting down ancient trees, polluting crystal clear streams, and leaving behind mountains of trash. Each image pulsed with his anger, a sharp contrast to the vibrant memories of the land as it had once been—untouched, thriving, sacred.

"They disrespect this land," Aluk declared, his voice firm. *"They take, they destroy. This is our home—ours to protect. But we will not seek them out. We will only protect what is ours."*

One of the younger males, Tahkan, stepped forward. His chest puffed out, and he slammed his fists against it with a resounding thud. His grunt was sharp and filled with anger. *"We should have done this long ago! The Elder's patience only makes us weak."*

The murmurs that followed were low and conflicted, a hum of discontent mixed with uncertainty.

Mora, an older female, broke from the clan, her silver-streaked hair glinting faintly in the moonlight. She met Aluk's glare head on, her gesture dismissive. *"The Elder has kept us safe for generations. His way has worked. You would risk war? For what? To prove your strength?"*

Aluk snarled, stepping closer to Mora as his growl rumbled through the clearing. He swept his gaze over the other Sasquatch, his eyes blazing. *"If the Elder will not act, then we must. Who will stand with us? Who will protect what is ours?"*

The clearing fell silent. The Sasquatch exchanged glances, their gestures, and low grunts carrying unease.

Tahkan stepped forward again, pounding his chest. His voice rose above the quiet, bold and unwavering. *"I will fight."*

Others stayed where they were, their eyes shifting toward the Elder.

The Elder rose from his seat slowly. His imposing figure

moved into the light, his presence undeniably dominant. When he spoke, his low grunt silenced even the restless murmurs.

Images filled the minds of the clan, sharp and unrelenting: hairless ones wielding red-breath and thundersticks, machines ripping apart the forest, the clan scattered and hunted. *"If you act rashly, this is what will come. Not safety. Not victory. Destruction."*

Mora stepped closer to the Elder, releasing a low, rumbling grunt. Her demeanor was composed yet resolute, every note resonating with the gravity of her message: *"The forest has always protected us. If we draw attention to ourselves, there will be no place to hide."*

Aluk's grunt deepened, the anger in his body unmistakable. His thought-images surged again, their intensity unwavering. *"We will not let them destroy what is ours. We will wait for them to come—but if they cross into our home, they will not leave."*

He turned to Matto and those who had joined him, his voice ringing with finality. *"If the Elder will not lead us, then we will lead ourselves. The hairless ones will learn. This land is ours."*

The Elder's expression did not falter. After a long silence, he gestured toward the depths of the sanctuary. His voice rumbled low. *"If you choose this path, you choose it without my blessing. But know this—when the forest cries out for justice, it will not need your anger to answer."*

Without hesitation, Aluk turned and stalked into the darkness, his followers close behind. Tahkan moved silently alongside Matto, his hulking frame seeming to merge with the forest's dense undergrowth. Matto glanced back once, his expression unreadable, before disappearing into the trees.

CHAPTER 3

The morning air in White Bear Lake carried a sharp chill, the kind that hinted at winter's fast approach. Leaves littered the ground in vibrant reds and oranges, crunching underfoot as Levi stepped out of his truck and onto the driveway of Rob's house. The place looked the same as always—neatly kept, the lawn trimmed short, and Rob's fiancée Bree's fall decorations dotting the porch: pumpkins, mums, and a hand-painted sign that read, "Welcome to Our Patch."

Levi let out a small laugh as he approached the front door and gave it three quick knocks.

The door swung open almost immediately, and Rob stood there, his broad frame blocking most of the doorway. His boyish grin was matched by the ever-present scruff on his jawline.

"Levi!" Rob greeted, stepping aside to let him in. "Right on time, as always. Guess I shouldn't be surprised."

"Someone's gotta be," Levi said, brushing past him into the entryway. The smell of freshly brewed coffee hit him first, followed by the faint aroma of breakfast bacon. "You ready to go, or is Bree still making you fold napkins?"

Rob laughed, running a hand through his short brown hair. "Nah, I got my escape papers signed this morning. She's busy packing up wedding stuff and said to go and enjoy myself."

"This is your last shot to hang with the guys before you tie the knot," Levi said, smirking.

Rob motioned for Levi to follow him into the kitchen, where a spread of toast, eggs, bacon, and coffee sat on the counter. "Help yourself," Rob said. "The twins texted—they're on their way. Carter too."

Levi grabbed a slice of toast, leaning against the counter. "You get the truck loaded?"

"Mostly," Rob said. "Kept it light since we've got that hike ahead. Just the essentials—pack, tents, a few lightweight camping chairs, and, of course, the cooler."

Levi raised an eyebrow. "You expect us to carry a loaded cooler four miles?"

"That's what teamwork's for," Rob said with a grin.

"We switch off. It's not that bad."

"Not bad for you maybe," Levi said, laughing.

The crunch of tires on the driveway caught their attention. Rob peered out the kitchen window. "That'll be the twins."

Moments later, the front door swung open, and Tyler and Tyson walked in without so much as a knock.

Tyson entered first, his outfit catching the light. He wore a bright orange windbreaker, orange-and-white sneakers, and slim black joggers that looked more suited for a runway than a trailhead. His appearance was as polished as his gear— his manicured goatee, closely cropped hair, and carefully groomed eyebrows all adding to his sharp, put-together look. His whole color-coordinated look screamed style over function.

"There's the man of the hour!" Tyson said, grinning as he clapped Rob on the shoulder. "You ready for one last hurrah before Bree's got you runnin' errands every Saturday?"

"Can't wait," Rob deadpanned, though his grin gave him away.

Tyler followed close behind, slightly shorter than his brother but with the same athletic build. Dressed in a well-worn hoodie, cargo pants, and scuffed hiking boots, his look reflected his laid-back personality. His hair was barely contained under a battered baseball cap, and his gait carried a casual, easy confidence.

"What's good, Levi?" Tyler said, nodding.

"Not much, Tyler," Levi said, nodding back.

Tyson spread his arms wide. "Y'all see this? Fresh gear. Best-dressed camper, hands down."

Levi smirked, giving Tyson a once-over. "You know we're going camping, right? Hope you don't cry when that fancy windbreaker gets snagged on a branch."

Rob snorted. "Or when those shoes hit mud."

Tyson waved them off. "Y'all just jealous you can't pull it off like me. Style and survival go hand in hand, gentlemen."

Tyler rolled his eyes as he grabbed a piece of toast from the counter. "Man, you're gonna be cryin' about scuffs by mile one."

"Style and survival, huh?" Levi said with a grin. "We'll see about that."

Hearing another car pull into the driveway cut the conversation short. Carter stepped out of his sedan, carrying a duffel bag and what looked like an older, slightly weathered tent bag draped across his back.

Levi opened the door before Carter could knock. "There he is."

Carter gave a faint smile. "Figured I'd be the last one here."

"You are," Rob said from the kitchen. "But it's fine. Coffee?"

"I'm good," Carter responded. "Let's just get moving."

The group gathered by Rob's dual-cab truck, buzzing with energy as they prepared to load up. Tyler darted toward the passenger door. "Shotgun!"

"Man, no one's fightin' you for it," Tyson said with a smirk as he climbed into the backseat. "Guess I'll take the throne back here."

Levi and Carter exchanged amused glances while tossing their packs into the truck bed. Levi eyed the cooler skeptically.

"You really think that thing's making it all the way up the trail?" he asked.

Rob smirked. "It's not walking itself. Like I said, we're all taking turns."

By the time Rob slid into the driver's seat, Tyler was scrolling through his playlist, muttering to himself. "Not this... too slow... oh, here we go." He tapped his phone decisively, and the opening riff of Stevie Wonder's *"Superstition"* filled the cab.

"Finally," Tyson said, nodding along. "A good choice for once. About time you picked somethin' decent."

"Relax," Tyler said with a grin. "This is just the opening act."

Levi leaned back in his seat, grinning. "Let's hope the opening act isn't better than the rest. We've got a long drive."

The truck pulled out of the driveway, the music lifting their spirits as they left White Bear Lake behind.

The drive was filled with music, jokes, and plenty of ribbing. Tyson leaned forward, glancing at Rob. "So, where exactly are we campin'? You've been all mysterious about it."

Rob smirked, his eyes still on the road. "It's a special place. My dad used to take me there all the time growing up. It's an old trailhead, barely used anymore. Quiet, secluded. Perfect for this kind of trip."

Levi raised an eyebrow. "Barely used? Sounds like we might have to clear the trail just to get there."

"It's not that bad. The last time I was up there was only four years ago," Rob replied. "You'll see—it's worth it."

Levi nodded as he gazed out the window, watching the dense forest blur past.

"Almost there," Rob said, knowing the directions by heart.

"Good," Tyson said, stretching his arms behind his head. "I've been savin' my energy for carryin' y'all on this hike."

"You're carryin' the cooler, not us," Tyler quipped. "And I don't think your gym routine's ready for that."

Laughter rippled through the cab as the truck finally pulled into a small clearing that served as a parking lot.

"All right," Rob said, pushing open the door and stretching. "Time to stretch those legs."

The group climbed out, the crisp forest air hitting their

faces as they stepped onto the dirt. Tyler was the first to grab his gear, slinging his pack over one shoulder with ease.

Tyson followed, hauling the cooler from the truck bed with a theatrical grunt. "This thing's a breeze," he said, grinning as he adjusted his grip. "All that gym work wasn't just to impress the ladies—it's for times like this."

Tyler raised an eyebrow. "Tyson, there are no women here. Unless you're tryin' to impress the squirrels, maybe save it."

"Y'all just jealous," Tyson shot back, flexing exaggeratedly before adding, "First shift's mine. Gotta show y'all how it's done."

"First shift's easy," Carter pointed out, pulling his worn pack onto his back. "Wait till you're carrying it on mile three."

"More like he'll be the first to drop it," Levi quipped, earning another laugh from the group.

Carter lingered by the truck, his eyes scanning the area. The parking lot was nearly empty, with just one other beat-up truck parked at the far end, its faded paint blending into the shadows of the surrounding trees. He frowned slightly. "Not many people here," he said, his tone cautious.

Levi glanced at him, then toward the trailhead. "Good. That means we've got the place mostly to ourselves. Less noise, more peace."

Carter nodded but didn't look entirely convinced.

Rob tightened the straps on his pack, giving it a firm tug as he surveyed the group. "It's about four miles to the campsite," he said. "Stay on the trail, keep a steady pace, and we'll rotate carrying the cooler every twenty minutes."

Without waiting for a reply, he stepped onto the trail. "Let's get moving," he called over his shoulder, setting a steady rhythm that the others quickly fell into.

The sounds of the forest—rustling leaves, distant birdcalls, and the occasional snap of a twig—blended with their quiet chatter. As they moved deeper, the trail narrowed, weaving through dense undergrowth and ancient trees.

Levi glanced back at Carter, who had remained unusually quiet. "You good back there?"

Carter looked up, startled. "Yeah. Just taking it all in."

Levi nodded, though Carter's tone, combined with his demeanor over the past twenty-four hours, didn't sit right with him.

Up ahead, Tyson's voice broke through the relative quiet. "Hey, how much farther? My majestic shoulders can only carry this beast so long."

Rob glanced back, smirking. "It's been eight minutes, Tyson."

The group burst into laughter, Levi chiming in, "Guess those gym sessions are just for show, huh?"

"Hey, carryin' this cooler builds character," Tyson shot back, feigning indignation. "Unlike some of you freeloaders."

Tyler rolled his eyes. "Quit whinin' and keep walkin'."

Their laughter echoed briefly as they took in the beauty of the surrounding wilderness.

CHAPTER 4

Deep in the Superior National Forest, near the edge of their territory where the ground dipped into dense thickets, three massive figures rested beneath the sprawling branches of an ancient oak. The darkness concealed their enormous shapes, merging them seamlessly with the shadowy woodland.

Aluk's broad chest rose and fell with the rhythm of sleep, his arms crossed over his powerful frame. Beside him, Matto's head rested against the tree trunk, his expression as still as the stone cliffs of their sanctuary. Tahkan, the youngest and most restless of the three, shifted in his sleep, his lips twitching as though chasing something in a dream.

A sudden gust of wind stirred the leaves above, carrying with it an unfamiliar scent. Tahkan's eyes snapped open. He sniffed the air, his nostrils flaring. The scent was faint but unmistakable—an intrusion, foreign and unwelcome.

He rose silently, his massive frame moving with the grace of a predator. Glancing once at the others to ensure they were still asleep, he followed the scent, weaving through the underbrush with ease. His long strides carried him swiftly over the uneven terrain.

For nearly two miles, Tahkan tracked the scent. It grew stronger with every step, mingled with traces of sweat, and something harshly chemical. His sharp ears picked up faint sounds: loud bursts of noise from unfamiliar voices. The sounds rose and fell in strange patterns that grated against the peaceful quiet of the woods.

Finally, he reached the crest of a hill overlooking a path winding through the trees. He crouched low, his bulky frame hidden by the thick brush, and peered down at the scene below.

A group of five hairless ones ambled along a trail, then came to a halt. They sat on large, uneven rocks scattered along the path, their strange bundles discarded nearby. One of them leaned back, emitting sharp, barking noises that carried across the forest. The rise and fall of these sounds reminded Tahkan of warning calls or challenges, but there was no urgency in the hairless one's movements.

Another reached into a small pouch at his waist, pulling out a slim object he placed in his mouth.

Tahkan's eyes narrowed. The hairless one flicked its hand, and a flash like a tiny bolt of lightning erupted. The object ignited, releasing curling tendrils of red-breath's shadow, its sharp, acrid scent invading the air.

The Sasquatch bristled, his hair standing on end. Red-breath. Memories of its red-tongues licking through the forest, consuming their sacred land, surged into his mind.

The other hairless ones didn't seem alarmed. They continued to bark sharply, their movements sluggish and uncoordinated.

Tahkan's fists clenched. His nostrils flared as frustration boiled over. Without thinking, he reached down and grabbed a small rock from the ground. He hurled it toward the group, the projectile ripping through the air.

The rock struck a tree just behind the hairless ones, its sharp crack silencing their noises.

The hairless ones glanced nervously at the treetops, their barking sounds replaced by uneasy silence.

Tahkan stayed perfectly still, his eyes narrowing. He hadn't wanted to be seen, only to disturb them, to force them to feel the unease they brought into the forest. He waited as they began to settle, seemingly oblivious to the eyes watching them.

When they moved on, he slipped away, retreating back into the forest.

The route to the tree was swift, his long strides devouring the ground as he moved through familiar terrain.

When he arrived, Aluk was already stirring, his amber eyes opening to slits as he caught Tahkan's scent approaching. Matto sat upright, his posture immediately alert.

Aluk let out a low grunt, the sound rolling through his chest like distant thunder. The meaning was clear: *"You left."* His gaze sharpened, edged with irritation.

Tahkan raised a hand, signaling for calm. Without a word, he projected sharp images into their shared consciousness: the hairless ones sitting on the path, their strange bundles, the shiny box of cold things. He lingered on the red-breath, its spark vivid in his thoughts, accompanied by the acrid smoke curling through the air.

A growl rumbled from Aluk's throat as the images solidified. His eyes snapped fully open, his body tensing like a coiled spring. *"They come closer every season. They do not stop."*

Matto rose to his feet, his face etched with alarm and frustration. A deep grunt, almost a question, reverberated: *"Where?"*

Tahkan gestured in the direction he had come, adding a sharp, clipped grunt to emphasize the distance. *"Two miles. Near the river trail."*

A knowing look exchanged between the brothers spoke volumes.

Aluk's massive frame loomed over the younger male as he unleashed a deep growl, low and heavy with promise. *"We will find them."*

Matto nodded, his broad shoulders tight. He motioned toward the woods, punctuating the gesture with a soft growl. *"But first, we feed the family."*

The three moved as one, their immense forms blending seamlessly into their surroundings as they tracked the faint scent of deer through the forest. The kill would be swift, the meat carried back to the caves before nightfall.

Then they would find the hairless ones. Tonight, the intruders would learn whose forest they had entered.

CHAPTER 5

After hours of trekking, the trail finally opened up into a small clearing, a perfect circle carved into the forest. Tall pines framed the space, their needle-covered branches forming a natural canopy. The group stepped into the clearing, the faint sound of a nearby stream accompanied by the scents of clean, crisp water and earthy soil filling the air.

"This is it boys," Rob said, letting his pack drop onto the mossy ground with a satisfying thud. He stretched his arms over his head, his back popping loudly. "Home sweet home for the weekend."

Levi stepped into the middle of the clearing, turning in a slow circle. "Not bad. Plenty of space for the tents, and that stream's close enough for water if we need it."

"Yeah, yeah," Carter said nonchalantly, scanning the clearing before dropping his pack beside Rob's. "But where's the bar?"

"Here," Tyson said, hefting the cooler off his shoulder with an exaggerated groan. He wiped imaginary sweat from his brow and gave the others a triumphant look. "Y'all see that? Strongest man in the group, reportin' for duty!"

"More like loudest," Tyler said, setting his own pack down smoothly.

Tyson shot him a mock glare. "Oh, I see how it is. I carry this beast for miles, and now you wanna talk slick?"

"Miles?" Tyler snorted. "We all offered to help, but no—you had to play superhero. Just showing off, as usual."

"Whatever," Tyson said, rolling his eyes. "You're just mad you can't lift it."

The group wasted no time unpacking their gear, their movements a blend of natural confidence from some and the awkward determination of those less familiar with the wilderness, all intent on making it their home for the next few days.

Rob unzipped his pack and pulled out a rolled-up tent. "All right, guys. Tents go here," he said, pointing to a flat section of the clearing. "Cooler stays by the fire pit—once we build one. Levi, you're on wood duty."

Levi saluted playfully. "On it."

Carter, already crouched beside his pack, frowned slightly. "Shouldn't we dig a fire pit or something first? Isn't that, like, a rule?"

Rob waved him off. "We're fine. This isn't our first camping trip, remember?"

"Yeah," Carter said under his breath, "but it's been a while."

"I got it," Tyson said, already clearing a patch of ground.

The group spread out, busy with their tasks. Levi disappeared into the woods, returning moments later with an armful of dry sticks and larger branches.

Tyler unrolled his tent with dramatic confidence, only to realize he'd somehow twisted it into a shape more resembling a tarp than a shelter.

"Need help?" Tyson asked, glancing up from the fire pit he was constructing.

"Nah, I got this," Tyler said confidently. Moments later, the tent collapsed on itself, drawing a round of laughter from the others.

"Classic," Levi said as he stacked the firewood into a neat pile near the cooler.

Meanwhile, Carter had already finished setting up his one-man tent with ease, the compact shelter standing neatly at the clearing's edge.

Rob finished staking down his tent and stood, surveying the site with satisfaction. The clearing was beginning to look like a proper campsite, with their tents forming a loose semicircle and the fire pit neatly arranged in the center.

"All right," Rob said, brushing his hands together. "Moment of truth—who's bunking where?"

"We've got three tents, right?" Levi asked, pointing to them.

"Yup," Rob said. "Two two-person tents and the little solo tent Carter brought."

"Called it!" Tyson said immediately, raising his hand. "I'm not sharin'. I need space for my majestic self."

"You mean your snorin'," Tyler said, rolling his eyes.

"Exactly," Tyson replied with a grin. "I'm doin' y'all a favor."

Rob sighed, shaking his head. "Fine. Tyson gets the solo tent. The rest of us are doubling up."

"I'll bunk with Tyler," Levi said, dragging his sleeping bag toward a tent.

Carter glanced at Rob, his expression neutral. "Guess that makes us tent buddies," he said quietly.

"Guess so," Rob replied. "As long as you don't mind me hogging the sleeping bag."

Carter managed a faint smile. "I'll survive."

As they set up their sleeping bags, Tyson pulled out his phone and frowned. "Man, I got no service out here."

Tyler glanced up from his tent. "What you need service for? You plannin' to call Mom?"

Tyson grinned. "Nah, but I was gonna post a selfie. Show people how real men rough it in the wild."

"Right," Levi said, smirking. "Because nothing says 'real men' like filtered selfies."

"Jealousy's a bad look, bro," Tyson shot back, slipping his phone into his pocket.

Once the camp was set up, the group gathered around

the fire pit, where Levi had begun arranging the wood into a neat pyramid after his second trip. Tyson crouched beside him, holding the match with an exaggerated pause.

"And here we have the modern caveman," he said, striking the match with flair before lighting the kindling. "Witness as he conquers nature itself."

The fire caught, crackling to life as the flames spread through the dry wood. Levi leaned back, satisfied.

"All right," Rob said, clapping his hands together. "What's for dinner, you ask? The finest cuisine money can buy: hot dogs and beer."

"Perfect," Tyler said, reaching for the cooler. He opened it with theatrical flair, pulling out a six-pack. "And just what the doctor ordered."

"Ah, I could go for a cold one," Carter said eagerly as Tyler handed him one.

As the sky deepened to shades of orange and purple, the group relaxed around the fire, their laughter mingling with the crackle of the flames. The clearing felt alive, the warmth of the fire pushing back the coolness of the evening air.

After a while, Carter stood, brushing off his pants.

"Where you going?" Rob asked, looking up.

"Just gonna take a quick walk," Carter said, his tone casual. "Stretch my legs, look around a bit. Have a smoke."

Tyler frowned slightly. "You sure that's a good idea? It's getting dark."

"Yes, Mom," Carter replied. "Just want to check out the area."

"Don't get lost," Tyler said, grinning. "We'll send the search party after you in the morning."

"Thanks," Carter said dryly. He grabbed a flashlight from his pack and stepped out of the clearing, his silhouette disappearing into the trees.

The remaining four exchanged brief glances before turning back to their tasks.

CHAPTER 6

Levi crouched by the fire pit, meticulously stacking sticks and kindling into a tight bundle designed to catch quickly. Nearby, Tyler rummaged through the cooler, tossing a pack of hot dogs toward Rob.

"Buns are in here too," Tyler announced, pulling out a plastic bag and holding it up like a trophy. "Good job," Rob said dryly as he caught the bag. "What do you want, a medal?"

"Wouldn't hurt," Tyler replied with a grin, cracking open another beer and plopping onto a nearby log.

The group settled into a familiar rhythm as they prepared dinner, their banter filling the clearing with bursts of laughter. Yet, even as the firelight warmed the space, an underlying tension lingered—an unspoken awareness that one of them was missing.

Levi skewered a hot dog onto a stick and held it over the fire. "Anybody else think Carter's been acting weird?" he asked, breaking the lull in conversation.

Tyson popped the tab on another beer with a quick motion. "Weird how? He's always actin' like he's too cool for the rest of us."

Levi frowned slightly, turning his stick over the flames. "It's not just that. He seems... distracted."

Tyler leaned back against the log, taking a swig of his beer. "Man barely said two words the whole hike. Usually, he'd be talking trash to Tyson by the halfway point."

"Hey!" Tyson protested, then shrugged. "Fair."

Rob, focused on turning his hot dog just right, finally spoke up. "He's probably just wiped. The hike was tougher than I remembered it to be, and Carter's not exactly the camping type."

"You think that's all it is?" Levi asked, glancing toward the woods where Carter had disappeared.

Tyson smirked. "Maybe he just needs to get laid."

Tyler snorted, nearly spilling his beer. "Ain't that the truth. Dude probably don't even remember what that's like."

Levi rolled his eyes. "I'm being serious. It's like he's got something on his mind."

Rob leaned forward, resting his forearms on his knees. "If it's something, he'll deal with it. Carter's not the type to bring anyone else into his problems."

"Exactly," Tyson said, holding up his can. "Man's got space now. Let him work it out. No need to make it some intervention or whatever."

Levi didn't reply, his gaze returning to the tree line. It was getting darker as the last traces of daylight faded, but there was still no sign of Carter's flashlight or movement.

Crickets sang softly, and the night buzzed with the quiet movement of small creatures. Somewhere in the distance, an owl hooted, its call oddly distorted.

"You hear that?" Tyson said, his voice dropping a little.

"Hear what?" Tyler asked, looking up from the fire.

"That owl. Sounds... off," Tyson said, frowning.

"Man, it's just an owl," Tyler replied, rolling his eyes.

"You're not about to say the woods are haunted or somethin', are you?"

Levi glanced at Tyson but said nothing. The unease pressing on him hadn't let up, and every sound seemed sharper now.

"Whatever," Tyson said, popping open another can. "At least the beer's cold. That's all that matters."

Rob chuckled, handing Tyler a hot dog on a stick. "And not burning these things."

"Thanks, man," Tyson said, biting into his hot dog with enthusiasm. "Let me finish this one, and then I'll cook the rest. Hauling that cooler with all my 'majestic' muscles worked up a serious appetite."

Tyler smirked as he leaned back against a log. "Majestic muscles, huh? I'm just surprised you didn't collapse halfway here, Mr. Gym Hero."

CHAPTER 7

Carter stepped into the tree line, the soft crunch of his boots muffled by the thick layer of pine needles. The beam of his flashlight bounced with each step as he lit a cigarette, the brief flicker of the lighter illuminating his face. He exhaled a long stream of smoke, watching it swirl and disappear into the cold night air.

The faint sounds of his friends' voices and the occasional pop of the campfire quickly faded as he moved deeper into the woods. The stillness was broken only by the soft sounds of nature: the wind in the trees and the trickling stream.

He swung the flashlight in lazy arcs, scanning the underbrush. He wasn't sure why he'd needed to get away—it wasn't like the others had done anything to annoy him. Maybe it was the unfamiliar setting, or it could have been the buildup of anxiety from everything he wasn't saying. Either way, he needed the space.

Carter stopped in a small clearing near the stream. The water glimmered faintly in the moonlight, rippling as it trickled over rocks. He crouched, setting his flashlight on a nearby boulder, and took another drag of his cigarette. The smoke mixed with the earthy scent of damp moss and fallen leaves.

Then he heard it: a low, soft hoot cutting through the stillness.

Carter listened intently, his gaze narrowing. A second hoot, lower and lingering, echoed with a sorrowful tone.

"Tyson," he mumbled under his breath, smirking slightly. "Always gotta mess with somebody."

It had to be Tyson. Classic move, trying to spook him just for kicks. Carter shook his head, carelessly tossing his cigarette butt into the stream and grabbing his flashlight. "Not buying it, man," he said as he started back toward camp.

But the woods had grown unnervingly quiet. The forest fell silent, replaced by an unusual stillness. Carter's pace quickened, his flashlight sweeping back and forth.

The hoots came again, this time from two directions.

Carter slowed, frowning. It didn't sound right—not quite like owls, but not entirely off, either. His smirk faded as unease prickled at the back of his neck.

"What are you scared of?" he mumbled, unconvinced. "It's just the guys screwing around."

He forced himself to keep walking, even as his anxiety grew. When he got to the clearing, the glow of the campfire and the familiarity of his friend's voices steadied his nerves. He stepped back into the light, shrugging off the unease like a heavy coat.

Tyson was the first to notice him. "About time!" he said, leaning back on the log. "You out there communin' with nature or somethin'?"

Carter headed for the cooler and cracked open a beer with one hand. "You guys think you're real funny, don't you?"

The group exchanged confused glances. "What are you talking about?" Rob asked.

Carter gestured vaguely toward the woods. "The hoots. Nice try, but it's gonna take more than that to freak me out."

Levi frowned. "We didn't do anything."

Tyler nodded, his brow lowering. "Yeah, man. We heard

that too. Creepy as hell, right?"

Carter paused mid-sip, his expression shifting. "Seriously? That wasn't you?"

"Nope," Tyson said, shaking his head. "And it wasn't just one. Sounded like a whole group." He paused, his brow furrowing. "What's a group of owls called anyway? A flock? That doesn't sound right. Maybe a hoot of owls?"

Levi glanced over, exasperated. "It's a parliament. A parliament of owls."

Tyson raised an eyebrow, clearly impressed. "A parliament? Man, that's fancy. Like they're sittin' around passin' laws or somethin'."

Tyler snorted. "Yeah, laws about who gets to eat mice first."

Carter forced a laugh as he sat down in one of the camping chairs. "Guess it's just owls, then," he said dismissively, though the flicker of doubt in his eyes betrayed him.

Levi watched him carefully. "You sure that's all it was?"

"Yeah," Carter said, waving him off. "What else would it be? Owls, birds—take your pick."

CHAPTER 8

Tyson leaned back, patted his belly with a satisfied grin, and let out a loud belch. "Man, that hit the spot," he said, reaching for his beer.

The fire burned low as the friends lounged around the fire pit, full and content from their dinner of hot dogs and beer. A few chuckled at Tyson's antics, while others lazily crushed empty beer cans underfoot or set them on the logs beside them.

"Yo, Tyson," Tyler said, pointing at his brother with a hot dog skewer. "You keep talkin' about 'precision cookin',' but these dogs look like you grilled them over a blowtorch."

Tyson grinned, jabbing the hot dog with his fork. "First off, that's called *flavor*. Second, remind me when the last time was that you touched a grill without almost settin' yourself on fire?"

"That was one time," Tyler shot back, his tone defensive but playful. "And I still say that grill was faulty."

"Faulty?" Levi said, cracking open another beer. "Pretty sure the only thing wrong that day was your brain. You were pouring lighter fluid on a gas grill."

The group erupted into laughter, Tyler included. He raised his beer in mock surrender. "Alright, alright. You've all got jokes tonight. Just don't come crying to me when Tyson burns breakfast."

"Breakfast? Please." Tyson waved at the remnants of dinner with a flourish. "I just served you all gourmet hot dogs. Gordon Ramsay himself would be knockin' on my door for a lesson."

Rob smirked, leaning back against a log. "Bree might disagree with that. She's pickier about her food."

"Oh, here we go," Tyler said, rolling his eyes. "The Rob-and-Bree show. Man, you've been talkin' about that girl all day."

Rob shrugged, a good-natured grin spreading across his face. "Can you blame me? Wedding's in two weeks. She's amazing. And this trip's kind of for her too."

"How's that?" Levi asked, leaning forward.

"She said I needed one last 'guys' trip,'" Rob replied, making air quotes. "You know, before I 'officially become a husband and leave behind all my single-boy shenanigans.'"

"Well," Tyler said, raising his can, "here's to Bree—marryin' Rob and puttin' up with his shenanigans."

They all laughed and toasted, clinking their cans together. Only Carter sat apart from the circle, nursing his beer in silence. Levi noticed and nudged him with his elbow.

"Hey, buddy. You good?" Levi asked.

Carter blinked, like he was being pulled out of a daze. "Yeah, I'm good. Just tired."

"You sure?" Tyler asked, giving him a sideways look. "You've got that 'zoned-out' face."

Carter managed a small smile, but it didn't quite reach his eyes. "Yeah, man. I'm good. Just thinking."

They let it go, the group easing back into their usual banter. Tyler launched into a story about a failed road trip, complete with an overly ambitious detour to see the world's largest ball of twine. Levi nearly spat out his beer when Tyler reenacted the group's dramatic fight over directions.

As the night deepened and the fire dimmed to glowing embers, Levi heard it first—the strange owl calls breaking the quiet again. He paused, his beer halfway to his mouth, and tilted his head to listen.

"You hear that?" he asked.

Rob looked up. "Hear what?"

"Owls again," Levi murmured, his brow lowering. "They sound... off."

The calls echoed once more, shrill and uneven, as if something unfamiliar was trying—and failing—to imitate a natural sound.

Tyson leaned forward, his frown deepening. "Yeah, that ain't right, man. Owls don't hoot like that."

"Yeah, I don't know." Rob said, glancing toward the darkness beyond the firelight. "Could be something else."

Tyson leaned back against the log, a beer resting on his knee as he listened to the distant hoots. "It has to be owls," he said, waving a hand. "They're just out here doing their thing. Probably some weird matin' call or somethin'."

"They sound broken," Tyler said, smirking. "Maybe they

need a little help."

Levi chuckled. "You volunteering, Tyler?"

"Hey, I'm just sayin'," Tyler replied with a grin, raising his beer in mock solemnity. "I'm a giver."

Carter rolled his eyes, taking a sip of his beer. "Right. Let's hear your best owl impression then."

Tyler leaned back and let out an exaggerated, guttural "Hoo-hoo!" that echoed into the woods, making Tyson burst into laughter.

"Man, that isn't even close!" Tyson said, clutching his stomach.

"Don't hate, little brother," Tyler shot back. "That right there? Owl-seduction gold."

Levi laughed, but his gaze shifted toward the trees, the humor doing little to settle his unease. "If that doesn't scare off whatever's out there, I don't know what will."

Carter didn't join in the laughter. He stared into the fire for a moment before shaking his head. "Probably just some dumb birds," he said, though his voice had a sharp edge to it. The others exchanged glances but didn't push.

"All right, I'll leave you men to the horny owls. I'm hitting the sack," Rob said, stretching with a tired groan.

"Yeah, feels like it's about that time," Levi agreed, picking up a few stray cans and tossing them into the cooler.

Tyler stood, grabbing a flashlight from his pack. "Gonna take a piss first. Ain't no way I'm riskin' some forest critter bitin' my manhood in the dark."

Tyson smirked. "How would they even find it?"

Tyler shot him a glare, but Tyson chuckled and stood up. "Relax, man. I'll join you. Safety in numbers, right?"

"Real comfortin'," Tyler muttered, shaking his head as the two disappeared toward the edge of the clearing.

Carter stood as well, stretching briefly. "I'm turning in too," he said quietly, heading toward the tents without another word.

"Don't wander too far," Rob called after Tyler and Tyson, closing the cooler. "We don't need any surprises out here."

CHAPTER 9

Levi shot up, feeling groggy and confused, the suffocating darkness of the tent enveloping him. He wasn't sure what had woken him at first—maybe the cold, maybe some half-forgotten dream. He blinked a few times, his body still caught between sleep and wakefulness, his mind sluggish. For a short while, he just lay there, staring at the faint outline of the tent's fabric.

Then the dull ache in his bladder became impossible to ignore.

"Dammit," he mumbled, fumbling for his flashlight.

He glanced over at Tyler, who was sprawled in his sleeping bag, snoring soundly, completely undisturbed. *"Lucky bastard,"* mused Levi as he crawled out of his sleeping bag.

The tent zipper rasped sharply as he tugged it open, stepping into the chilly embrace of the October night. The campfire had dwindled to faintly glowing embers, their soft glow barely illuminating the clearing. The cold air hit him like a blade, crisp and biting, prompting him to pull his hoodie tighter against the shiver that ran through him.

The campsite was strangely still. There were no sounds of crickets or wind, no faint animal calls—just silence. Levi didn't notice at first, his half-asleep brain too focused on his desperate need to pee. He shuffled to the border of the camp, his boots crunching faintly on the dry leaves scattered across the ground.

He reached a spot just beyond the tents, far enough to avoid any awkward morning complaints, and released a long sigh as he relieved himself. His breath was visible in the cold air, curling upward in pale clouds. An unnatural hush cloaked the forest, the kind that made the hair on the back of his neck prickle. It wasn't until he zipped up his pants that the eerie stillness truly sank in.

It's too quiet, he thought.

Levi frowned, glancing around the dark forest surrounding the camp. The quiet wasn't peaceful; it was heavy, unnatural.

Then he heard a sharp snap, the unmistakable sound of a twig breaking underfoot.

Levi stopped instantly, his breath catching in his throat. The sound had come from somewhere to his right, just beyond the dim light of the fire. He squinted through the darkness, but the trees were nothing more than black shapes against the night sky.

A low, deep growl followed, short but resonant, vibrating in the cold air. Levi's chest tightened. A bear, he thought immediately. *Shit.*

He forced himself to stay still, his pulse hammering in his ears. His flashlight was still clutched in his fist, but he didn't dare turn it on. The last thing he wanted was to startle whatever was out there.

Levi retreated slowly, taking care not to stumble over anything. His boots crunched faintly on the forest floor, and he winced at the sound, his heart racing.

Don't run. Just back away. Slowly.

He took another step, his eyes locked on the tree line, straining to catch any sign of movement. The growl didn't come again, but the quietness didn't lift either. Every instinct screamed at him to turn and bolt, but he knew better.

His tent was only a few steps away now. He resisted the urge to glance over his shoulder, keeping his focus forward as he walked backward toward the safety of his tent.

When he finally ducked inside, zipping the flap closed behind him, he released a shaky breath. Tyler lay beside him, his snoring steady and soft, still deeply asleep. Levi sank into his sleeping bag, his body stiff with anxiety, his ears straining for any sound from outside.

But the forest remained soundless, the absence of noise truly unnerving. Levi's mind raced, replaying the moment over and over. The growl had been deep and guttural, primal in a way that set his nerves on edge. *Bears growled like that, didn't they? It had to be a bear. What else could it be?*

He adjusted his position, wincing at the rustle of his sleeping bag. Tyler mumbled something about twinkie rolls in his sleep but didn't wake, rolling onto his side with a soft sigh.

The minutes ticked by, stretching into what felt like hours. Levi lay still, his body still tense, his breathing shallow. He stared at the ceiling of the tent, trying to calm his beating heart. *Why do I feel so scared?* He pondered silently. *I'm familiar with the woods, seen countless bears. What the hell?* He thought.

Then, gradually, the world seemed to come back to life. The faint chirping of crickets returned, hesitant at first but growing steadier. Levi exhaled slowly, his heart rate finally beginning to slow. Whatever had been out there was gone now—at least, he hoped so.

He closed his eyes, willing himself to relax. It took nearly half an hour, but eventually, the exhaustion of the day won out, and his body gave in. His breathing evened out as sleep finally claimed him.

CHAPTER 10

The first light of dawn crept over the forest, bathing the campsite in muted gray. Tyson stirred awake, blinking groggily before unzipping the tent and stepping into the cool October morning. He yawned deeply, stretching as his breath fogged in the crisp air.

As he glanced around, his muscles froze mid-stretch. His eyes widened as they swept across the clearing.

"Man, who did *this*?" Tyson's voice, loud and sharp, broke the morning silence.

Levi stirred in his sleeping bag, groaning as the noise dragged him from sleep. "What's going on?" he called, his voice muffled by the tent walls.

The others began to wake, fumbling to get out of their sleeping bags. Tyler was the first to stick his head out. "Man, you better have a good reason for yelling this early," he grumbled, rubbing his face.

"You gotta see this," Tyson said, his tone tight.

Levi climbed out of his tent after Tyler, pulling his hoodie tighter against the chill. Rob and Carter followed, shaking off their grogginess as their eyes landed on what Tyson had discovered.

The campsite was a disaster.

The camp chairs were scattered across the clearing, one of them bent and lying on its side. Beer cans, some crushed and others still half-full, littered the dirt. The cooler had been overturned, its contents—leftover hot dogs, drinks, and snacks—strewn everywhere.

"What the hell happened?" Rob asked, stepping closer to the overturned cooler.

"Looks like a bear," Carter offered, though his voice was hesitant.

"A bear?" Levi crouched near the cooler, frowning. "I don't think so."

"Why not?" Tyler asked, gesturing at the mess. "This is exactly what a bear would do, right?"

Levi ran his hand over the cooler's latch, inspecting it. He looked up at Rob, his expression serious. "You locked the cooler last night, right?"

Rob nodded firmly. "Yeah, I double-checked before going to bed."

Levi brushed some dirt off his hands and pointed at the cooler. "If it were a bear, there'd be claw marks. The lid would be shredded or ripped off completely. This? It was unlatched, like someone just...opened it."

Carter folded his arms. "So you're saying it wasn't a bear? Then what else could it be?"

Levi stood, his face grim. "A bear doesn't have opposable thumbs. Whatever opened this did it deliberately."

The group exchanged uneasy looks. Rob glanced toward the edge of the woods, his confidence faltering. Levi's words left a heavy unease in the air.

"Wait," Tyson said suddenly, his tone sharp as his eyes scanned the group. "One of y'all didn't get up last night, did you? Had a few too many and started messin' with stuff?"

"Nope," Carter said flatly. "Slept like a rock."

"Not me," Tyler added, shaking his head. "I didn't move once I got in my bag."

"Same here," Rob said. "Didn't hear or see anything."

Levi's voice was steady but firm. "Then it wasn't us. And it sure wasn't a bear."

Carter let out a sharp breath. "So what? You think someone else was out here? Another person?"

"Someone—or something," Levi replied, his tone measured.

"Maybe it was some punks," Tyler said, though he sounded less confident now. "Kids messing around, trying to freak people out."

Tyson scoffed, shaking his head. "Man, ain't nobody hikin' *this* deep into the woods just to prank some campers. Be for real. Only thing I can see is other hikers—maybe drunk, maybe high—but even that don't make sense."

The surrounding forest buzzed with the sounds of small animals starting their morning, a sharp contrast to the unease hanging over the group.

"What are you thinking, Levi?" Rob asked.

All eyes turned to Levi, who shifted uncomfortably. "I got up to pee last night," he admitted, his voice hesitant. "Heard a twig snap, then this low growl. I thought it was a bear, so I just backed off and went back to my tent. Figured it wandered off."

"And you didn't think to wake us?" Rob snapped, his frustration clear.

"What was I gonna do? Wake everybody up to say I heard a bear?" Levi shot back. "Bears are common out here. Didn't seem like it was worth disturbing everyone."

The group exchanged uneasy looks as the morning chill seemed to bite a little deeper.

Tyson, still pacing through the mess, suddenly stopped. "Yo, who left all the food in the cooler?" he asked, pointing to a torn bag near the edge of the clearing.

Everyone turned to look at the shredded bag of chips, its contents scattered across the dirt. Levi frowned. "We didn't leave those out. Did we?"

Tyson's frustration bubbled over. "I told y'all last night—everythin' goes in the pack up the tree. We can't just leave food in the cooler. Now we got animals—or whatever this is—rummagin' through our stuff."

Levi sighed, rubbing the bridge of his nose. "Alright, from now on, everything—every last scrap of food—gets tied in the tree. No exceptions. This can't happen again."

Tyler raised his hands in mock surrender. "Fine, fine, Captain Safety."

"Good," Levi said firmly. "Because next time, we might not just be cleaning up a mess."

They spent the next while cleaning up the wreckage, their usual banter replaced by a strained silence. Tyson tried cracking a few jokes, but they fell flat, his usual confidence replaced by nervous energy.

As they reset the camp, Levi couldn't shake the feeling that they were being watched. His eyes kept darting to the edge of the woods, his gut twisting with unease.

It had to be a bear, he told himself, trying to bury the doubt creeping into his thoughts. Other campers seemed unlikely. What else could it be?

Although the camp appeared to be back to its usual state, a persistent, unsettling feeling remained.

CHAPTER 11

Hidden among the dense trees, their forms melded so perfectly with the forest that they were nearly invisible. Their dark hair, damp with morning dew, blended with the bark and shadows, while their sharp eyes remained focused on the hairless ones bustling in the clearing below.

Tahkan crouched low, his lean frame stiff with anticipation. Frustrated, he turned to Aluk, the biggest of the three, and emitted a low groan, pounding his chest twice as if to ask, *"Why didn't we act last night?"*

Aluk straightened, his towering form radiating authority. He turned his head slowly toward Tahkan, narrowing his dark eyes. With a low growl and a deliberate hand gesture—a slow sweep of his massive arm toward the hairless ones—he conveyed *patience*. His clawed hand then tapped his own temple, the universal signal among their kind for think first.

Tahkan huffed quietly, his annoyance evident. He gestured sharply toward the hairless ones, his hand mimicking their movements: *walking, laughing, oblivious.* His meaning was clear. *They were vulnerable.*

Aluk responded with a deep, guttural grunt that shook the trees. His powerful hand clamped down on Tahkan's shoulder as he leaned closer, his mind sending an image directly into the younger one's thoughts: a hairless one holding a long, shiny weapon—one of their dreaded thundersticks. The image shifted, showing a Sasquatch falling, blood soaking into the earth.

Tahkan flinched at the vividness of the image and growled softly in protest, shaking his head. He gestured rapidly with both hands, fingers clawed in frustration. *They didn't have them. I didn't see any thundersticks.*

Aluk emitted a low rumble of disapproval, his hand curling into a fist. His response was swift and firm, both through gestures and mental projection. *Not seeing doesn't mean they don't have them. Acting without knowing is foolish.*

Nearby, Matto—the stockiest of the three—watched with quiet amusement. He stepped forward, his silver-streaked chest hair catching the morning light. With a snort and a dismissive flick of his hand, he sent *Tahkan an image of himself recklessly blundering into danger, only to be struck down by a crack of thunderstick. The image ended with Tahkan sprawled lifeless on the ground.* Matto's deep, rumbling chuckle followed, dark with mockery.

Tahkan snarled softly, his pride stung. He jabbed a finger toward the camp again, his hand miming the hairless ones' laughter and careless behavior. His gestures and a brief mental projection conveyed his frustration. *They are weak, unprepared. We should take them now.*

Aluk's eyes hardened, and he raised a hand sharply, commanding silence. He leaned closer, sending an unmistakable image into Tahkan's mind: *the hairless ones huddled together, fear in their eyes, their movements slow and hesitant. One by one, they were picked off, isolated, and overwhelmed.*

Through his gestures and mental projection, Aluk conveyed the plan. Not now. Later. We wait. Let them doubt. Let them fear. Then, we act. One by one.

Tahkan lowered his head, chastened but still restless. He glanced back at the camp, where the hairless ones were unaware of the eyes watching them. Aluk, satisfied that his message had been received, turned to Matto and gestured toward the forest with a series of short, deliberate movements. *Hunt. Feed the clan. Prepare for tonight.*

Matto nodded, grunting his agreement. He motioned for Tahkan to follow, a sharp flick of his hand signaling the direction they would take. *The stream. There will be deer.*

Tahkan paused briefly, then joined Matto, his long limbs gliding with stealth. They disappeared into the trees, leaving Aluk behind, his massive form becoming one with the surroundings.

He crouched low, his piercing gaze locked on the hairless ones below. With a soft growl, he projected an image into his own mind: the camp in chaos, the hairless ones scattering into the night, their fear overwhelming. His lip curled in satisfaction.

They would learn soon enough. This was not their forest. It belonged to the clan.

With that, Aluk rose silently and moved into the deeper woods, his massive frame vanishing into the mist. The forest seemed to stir in his wake, the faint creak of swaying branches and the murmur of a distant stream filling the still air.

The hairless ones had one more day of ignorance. Tonight, the forest would remind them who truly ruled its shadows.

CHAPTER 12

The morning's chill had given way to the golden warmth of a perfect autumn day. The group packed up their fishing gear, grabbed the cooler of beer, and set off into the woods, eager to leave the earlier unease behind them.

"Alright," Tyson said, hefting the cooler onto his shoulder, "time to catch some dinner. I don't care if it's a guppy or a sea monster—we're eatin' good tonight."

"Sea monster?" Levi asked, smirking as he adjusted his hold on the rod. "You do realize we're in Minnesota, right?"

"Call it optimism, man," Tyson replied, grinning. "Gotta aim high."

"Or aim at all," Tyler quipped. "You couldn't catch a fish if it swam into your net."

The group laughed, their spirits lifting as they made their way deeper into the woods. The trail wound through the forest, past towering pines, and patches of fiery orange and gold. Birds flitted overhead, their songs creating a peaceful backdrop to the group's chatter.

As they reached a rise in the trail, the trees opened up to reveal a small, crystal-clear lake nestled in the hollow below. The sunlight danced across the water's surface, making it shimmer like glass.

"Damn," Tyson said, dropping his bag to the ground. "That's gorgeous."

"This is Devil Track Lake," Rob said, gesturing toward the water. "My Dad used to bring me out here to fish when I was growing up."

"Devil Track Lake?" Tyson asked, his eyebrows shooting up. "Why's it called that? Sounds like the start of a horror movie."

Rob shrugged, moving nearer to the water's edge. "I dunno. He never told me. Probably some old legend or something."

"Legends don't start with nice things," Tyson said, cracking open a beer. "You never hear about *Happy Angel Creek* or *Good Vibes Pond.* It's always Devil-this or Death-that."

"You'll be fishing on it, though," Levi pointed out with a smirk. "Guess you're not that worried."

Tyson grinned, raising his can in mock toast. "Hey, if the devil's out there, I'll catch him too. Someone's gotta put him on a hook."

The group chuckled and made their way toward the lake, but as they passed through a patch of tall cattails and scattered wild grass, Tyson suddenly stopped short.

"What in the hell is that?" Tyson asked, his voice low.

The others turned, following his gaze. Half-hidden in the weeds was a skeleton, its bleached-white bones stark against the weeds. As they stepped closer, it became clear that it had once been a deer. Most of the body had been picked clean, the ribs protruding upward like the frame of a broken umbrella.

"Whoa," Levi said, crouching down for a closer look. "That's... weird."

"What's weird about it?" Tyler asked, standing a few feet back. "It's nature, man. Stuff dies out here."

"No, look at the head," Levi said, pointing.

The group leaned in, their expressions shifting from curiosity to unease. The deer's skull was twisted unnaturally, the neck snapped in a way that made the head face completely backward.

"Okay, that's creepy," Rob said, taking a step back. "What could've done that?"

"A bear?" Carter suggested, though his tone lacked conviction.

"Bears don't do that," Levi said firmly. "They'll maul a carcass, sure, but they don't snap necks like that. And this wasn't eaten by a bear either—look at how clean the bones are. Whatever did this... it wasn't normal."

"You think it was people?" Tyler questioned, his voice tinged with nervous humor. "Could be poachers."

"I doubt it," Levi said, standing up and brushing his hands on his jeans. "No signs of tools, no cuts on the bones. But honestly, I have no idea what could've done this."

The group stood in silence for a short time, as they glanced around. Tyson broke the tension with a nervous laugh.

"Well," he said, stepping back from the skeleton, "whatever it was, it's not here now. Let's move on before I start hearin' banjos."

"Agreed," Rob said, turning back toward the trail.

When they finally reached the lake, the sight of the crystal clear water lifted their spirits again. They spread out along the shoreline, casting their lines and cracking open beers. The group's initial discomfort disappeared as they found a comfortable groove.

"Alright," Tyson called out from his spot on a rock, his line dangling lazily in the water. "What's the secret to catching fish? You gotta sing to 'em, or what?"

"Try being quiet for once," Tyler called back. "Fish don't like your voice, bro."

"Man, you're just mad I'm gonna catch the biggest one," Tyson shot back, grinning as he raised his beer in a mock toast.

The hours passed in a blur of laughter and friendly ribbing. Levi caught the first fish of the day—a decent-sized walleye—which earned him exaggerated applause from the group. Tyson, true to form, spent most of his time untangling his line from underwater snags, much to everyone's amusement.

By late afternoon, the group had caught enough fish for dinner and shared enough beers to feel a pleasant buzz. The hike back to camp was filled with jokes and stories, and who was the best fisherman.

As they trudged along the trail, Tyler held up his stringer proudly. "I'm just sayin'—this walleye right here? It's practically a trophy."

Tyson scoffed, shaking his head. "Man, that's bait compared to my pike. Look at this thing—it's almost too big for the pan."

Levi chuckled. "Y'all are dreaming. Everyone knows I landed the best one today."

Carter, walking at the rear of the group, smirked as he took a sip of his beer. "Sure, Levi. We all saw you fight that walleye like it was some prehistoric beast. Thought it was gonna pull you in."

Rob grinned, adjusting the pack slung over his shoulder. "Let's be real—none of you amateurs would've caught a thing without my expert guidance. I'm the only one here who knows what he's doing."

The group erupted in laughter, their voices echoing

through the trees. Tyson clapped Rob on the back, grinning. "Guidance? Then how come the *expert* has the smallest fish?"

Rob smirked, unfazed. "Because I was too busy making sure *you* clowns didn't scare all the fish away."

CHAPTER 13

As the group approached camp, their mouths watered at the thought of fresh fish cooked over the fire. Dinner was going to be the highlight of the day, and they couldn't wait to dig in.

"See?" Tyson said, dropping his gear onto the ground with a confident smirk. "Told y'all, nothin' to worry about."

"Yeah," Tyler shot back, shrugging off his pack. "The only thing we have to worry about is your cookin'."

The group chuckled. Tyson rolled his eyes but couldn't suppress a grin. "You're just mad you didn't get seconds last time."

Everything was just as they'd left it—tents upright, stack

of firewood still neatly arranged and no sign of disturbances.

"Alright," Rob said, rubbing his hands together. "We've got fish to clean and a fire to start. Who's doing what?"

"I'll handle the fish," Tyson volunteered, grabbing the bag of their catch. "You'd just mess it up anyway, Ty."

"Excuse me?" Tyler retorted, his voice growing louder. "I'll have you know I've cleaned fish before."

"Oh yeah?" Tyson shot back, grinning as he headed toward the spring a short distance from camp. "Last time you tried, you gagged so hard you almost puked."

"That fish smelled like feet, and you know it," Tyler said, following reluctantly. "I'll supervise this time, make sure you don't screw it up."

Carter stepped forward, grabbing his knife from his gear. "I'll help. More hands, less work."

"See?" Tyler said, throwing an arm over Carter's shoulder. "Team effort. I knew you'd come around, bro."

Levi chuckled as the three disappeared toward the spring, their voices carrying back to camp as they argued over the best way to clean fish.

"That's gonna take longer than it should," Rob remarked,

shaking his head.

"Guaranteed," Levi replied, crouching by the fire pit and starting to arrange the wood and kindling.

"You need a hand?" Rob asked, kneeling beside him.

"Yeah, if you could grab that stack of kindling over there," Levi said, nodding toward a pile of twigs and bark. Together, they worked efficiently, soon coaxing a small flame to life.

As the fire crackled to life, the thought of cooking over it stirred anticipation. There was nothing like food cooked over an open flame—the smoky aroma, the way it tasted richer, better, as if the fire itself added something no kitchen ever could.

By the time Tyler, Tyson and Carter returned with the cleaned fish, the fire was crackling steadily. Carter plopped down onto one of the camping chairs, looking flushed but happy, a fresh beer already grasped in his hand.

Levi's gaze lingered on him briefly.

"Fish are ready," Tyson announced, holding up the cleaned filets proudly. "You're welcome."

"Good man," Levi said, pulling out a small skillet from

his gear.

As Levi cooked the fish over the fire, he added sliced potatoes to the skillet, seasoning them with a pinch of salt and pepper. The aroma of sizzling butter, fish and potatoes soon filled the air, drawing appreciative murmurs from the group.

"Damn, Levi," Tyler said, sniffing the air. "You're out here cookin' like we're at a five-star restaurant."

"Don't let it go to his head," Tyson teased. "He'll start chargin' us for dinner."

"Hey, good food's worth it," Rob said, leaning back in his chair and cracking open a fresh beer. "This smells incredible."

"You know what?" Tyler said, grinning at Levi. "Abby must eat *real* good with you around. Bet she's spoiled."

Levi laughed, flipping the potatoes in the skillet. "She does alright. But don't let her hear you say that. She's been learning to cook, and she'll start thinking I'm critiquing her every meal."

"She's lucky, man," Tyson said, leaning back in his chair. "If I could make food that smelled this good, I'd get myself a good woman in no time."

He paused, then smirked as a thought crossed his mind. "On second thought, maybe not. Look at Rob—getting' married sounds more like a prison sentence."

Rob glanced up from his plate, unfazed. "Enjoy your freedom while it lasts, Tyson. You're next."

The group chuckled, and Tyson shook his head, grinning. "Nah, man. I'll stick to cookin' for myself. Way less headaches."

With the meal prepared, the group relaxed, enjoying their food as the camp echoed with satisfied chewing, grunts, and the occasional belch. Conversation faded as they focused on their plates, savoring the meal with the kind of enthusiasm only fresh-caught fish and campfire cooking could inspire.

"This," Rob said, raising his can in a toast, "is what it's all about. Good friends, good food and the stars above us. Doesn't get better than this."

"Hell yeah," Tyson said, raising his own can. "Amen to that."

The firelight flickered across their faces as they leaned back, enjoying the food and the quiet peace of the wilderness. The fish was perfectly cooked, its flaky texture enhanced by the crisp, buttery potatoes.

As the conversation lulled, Levi looked over at Rob with a thoughtful smile. "Hey, who here's known Rob the longest?"

Tyson and Tyler both looked at Carter, who shrugged casually, his beer resting on his knee. "That'd be me."

"Yeah, that tracks," Rob said, grinning. "We grew up on the same block. Carter was the first kid I met when my parents moved to the neighborhood."

Carter used to be a little terror," Rob added, shaking his head. "Always climbing trees, sneaking into places he shouldn't, pulling pranks on the neighbors."

"Still getting' into trouble, man?" Tyler asked, smirking.

"Not usually," Carter replied, his voice flat but with a faint smile.

"Man," Tyson said, laughing, "so you've known Rob longer than anyone here, and you're not roastin' him more? What's the point of all that history if you're not usin' it?"

Rob chuckled, his expression softening as he glanced at Carter. "Nah, Carter's not much of a roaster. But I'll give him credit—he's had my back more times than I can count."

"Like when?" Tyler pressed, leaning forward with a grin. "Come on, let's hear it."

Rob hesitated for a second, then smiled. "Alright, here's one. We were, what, nine? Walking home from school one day, and this group of older kids decided I was an easy target. They started pushing me around, calling me names. I just stood there—didn't know what to do."

Levi leaned in, intrigued. "What happened?"

"Carter happened," Rob said, grinning at his friend. "He didn't even hesitate. Walked right up to them, all five feet of him at the time, and told them to back off."

"They didn't listen, though," Carter said, shaking his head.

"No, they didn't," Rob agreed. "One of them shoved him, and Carter decked the kid. Full-on punch to the face. Dropped him right there. The rest of them scattered after that."

The group burst out laughing, and even Carter cracked a smile.

"Damn," Tyson said. "Carter, the neighborhood vigilante. I like it."

"Something like that," Rob said. "I owe him for that. And

for not letting me forget it every chance he gets."

Carter shrugged, taking another sip of his beer. "What can I say? I'm just a guy looking out for his buddy. And maybe knocking a few bullies down when they deserve it."

The group erupted into laughter again, the sound echoing into the night.

Just as the laughter started to fade, a long, haunting howl echoed through the night. It started low and deep, rising into a pitch that sent chills down their spines.

Instantly, the group looked up in the direction of the noise.

"Was that a wolf?" Carter asked, breaking the silence.

"No," Levi said, his voice quiet but firm. "It didn't sound like a wolf. It sounded... I don't know... almost like a siren."

"That was spooky as hell, man," Tyson said.

The group exchanged uneasy glances. For a short while, no one spoke.

"Probably a coyote," Rob said finally, forcing a chuckle. "Or some animal. We're in the woods after all."

The others nodded, slowly relaxing back into their

chairs. Tyler cracked open another beer, muttering, "Weird, though."

Baffled but unwilling to let the strange sound ruin their evening, they continued chatting and drinking, the firelight dancing in their eyes.

CHAPTER 14

The October air was crisp, but the warmth of their shared meal, alcohol, and company made the chill seem insignificant. Above them, stars dotted the sky, clearer than anyone had seen in a long time.

Rob leaned back in his chair, nursing the last of his beer. He'd been quiet for a while, a faint grin tugging at the corners of his mouth. It was the kind of grin that said he had something up his sleeve.

"Alright, fellas," Rob said, breaking the comfortable silence. "I've got a little something special for tonight."

"What are you talkin' about?" Tyson asked, sitting up with interest. "You holdin' out on us?"

"Maybe," Rob said, standing and moving toward his tent. "You know, it's my bucks. Gotta keep a few surprises."

Tyson's eyes lit up as he looked around the clearing with exaggerated excitement. "Wait a minute. Strippers? Are there strippers? Tell me there are strippers!"

Rob turned back, rolling his eyes. "You idiot. We're in the middle of the woods. Where exactly would I hide strippers?"

The group burst out laughing, and Levi shook his head. "I don't know, Rob. He seems awfully hopeful."

"Man, I'm just sayin'," Tyson said, grinning. "Would've been one hell of a surprise!"

Rob chuckled, pulling something out of his tent. "Sorry to disappoint. But no strippers. Just this."

He held up a bottle of *Weller 12 Year Bourbon Whiskey*, its amber liquid catching the firelight. "Figured we'd toast the weekend properly."

The laughter turned to cheers as Rob brought the bottle near the fire, passing it around. Tyson shook his head, still grinning. "Fine. No strippers. But this? This'll do."

The reaction was immediate. Tyler whistled, Tyson leaned forward with raised eyebrows, and Carter, who had been reserved all night, finally cracked a faint smile.

"Are you serious?" Levi asked, leaning forward. "That stuff's legendary."

"I know," Rob said with pride. "My old man gave me one of his bottles as a gift for the bucks. Figured now was the perfect time to crack it open."

"Hell yeah!" Tyson said, grabbing cups. "Why didn't you tell us sooner?"

"Had to save it for the right moment," Rob said.

"Let's get into it, then!" Tyson said eagerly.

Rob looked around the group, his grin faltering when Levi shook his head. "Nah, I'm good."

The others turned to him, surprised.

"You're passing on this?" Tyler asked. "Dude, this isn't some gas station six-pack. It's a once-in-a-lifetime whiskey."

"I know," Levi said with a shrug. "But someone's gotta keep their wits about them out here. I'll stick to water. You guys enjoy."

Rob smirked. "Fair enough. More for us."

He grabbed the bottle and twisted at the cap, only to stop with a grimace. "Ah, damn it. Gonna need a knife."

"You don't have one?" Tyson asked, exasperated.

"Nope. Carter, where's your knife?"

Carter, lounging back in his chair, gestured lazily toward the tents. "It's in my backpack. Front pocket."

"Perfect," Rob said, passing the bottle to Tyson. "Hold this."

He headed toward Carter's tent, ducking inside and unzipping the bag. His fingers searched the front pocket, brushing against the familiar cold metal of the knife. Just as he was about to pull it out, something else caught his attention—a smooth, delicate object. He frowned, pulling it free.

In the faint light, he saw it—a bracelet. Silver chain links adorned with small green stones. His chest tightened.

It was Bree's.

Rob's hand trembled as he held it up, the firelight catching on the stones. His mind reeled. This wasn't just a piece of jewelry—it was the bracelet he'd designed and given her last year for their anniversary. He remembered the way she'd smiled when she fastened it on her wrist. And now, somehow, it was in Carter's bag.

Rob's hand shook as he clenched the bracelet, the firelight dancing off its delicate silver links and green stones. His chest tightened, each breath heavier than the last as his mind raced with questions and accusations.

Walking slowly back to the fire, Rob's expression darkened, the bracelet clenched tightly in his fist. The chatter around the fire dwindled as the others noticed his demeanor shift.

"You good, man?" Tyler asked cautiously, setting down his beer.

Rob ignored him, his eyes fixed on Carter. He held up the bracelet, his voice slicing through the tension like a blade. "Carter. What the fuck is this?"

Carter looked at the bracelet, his face going pale for a split second before a cocky smirk settled on his lips. He leaned back slightly, crossing his arms. "It's a bracelet, Rob," he said casually, shrugging. "Relax."

Rob's jaw tightened as he stepped closer. "This isn't *just* a bracelet, you asshole. This is Bree's. *I* designed this. Every link, every stone. Why the fuck is it in your bag?"

Carter's smirk wavered momentarily before returning. "How am I supposed to know? Maybe she left it in my car, and it got mixed up. It's not like I took it. Damn you jump to conclusions easily."

"You're such a goddamn liar," Rob snapped, his voice climbing with rage. "This isn't some random mistake. You were supposed to be my best friend! You and Bree never hang out—you barely even talk to each other unless I'm there. And now you're telling me she left this in your car, and it somehow ended up in your *camping backpack*? Do you even hear how fucking ridiculous that sounds?"

Carter stood, the cockiness melting into frustration. "Rob, come on. Don't blow this out of proportion—"

"Blow this out of proportion?" Rob's voice cracked with rage as he stepped closer. "You've been fucking my fiancée, haven't you?"

"Rob!" Levi stepped forward, his voice firm. "Take a second to calm down."

But Rob wasn't listening. His fury boiled over, and he shoved Carter hard in the chest, sending him stumbling backward. "How long, Carter? How fucking long?"

Carter straightened, his jaw clenched. "Look, man, it's not what you think."

"Stop lying!" Rob roared, his voice breaking with anger. "Just fucking admit it already! You're such a piece of shit."

Carter's face twisted, a mix of anger and desperation overtaking him. Finally, the words burst out. "Fine! I saw her at a bar one night, Rob!" His voice carried through the clearing, raw and bitter. "We were both out, just by chance. We started talking, decided to have a drink together. One thing led to another, and... it happened, alright? After that..." He hesitated, his voice dropping. "It just kept happening. We couldn't stop. I couldn't stop."

The confession was a gut punch, leaving only stunned silence in the camp.

"It just kept happening?" Rob's voice was low and trembling. "Are you fucking serious?"

"Rob, I didn't want to hurt you, alright? I wanted to tell you, but Bree said it'd destroy you. She begged me not to. I—"

Rob's fist connected with Carter's jaw before he could finish, the impact sending him staggering back. Carter recovered quickly, swinging wildly and catching Rob on the cheek. The two collided, fists flying in a blur of rage and betrayal.

"Stop it!" Levi yelled, rushing forward to pull Rob away.

Tyson joined him, grabbing Carter by the shoulders and shoving him back.

"Enough!" Tyson barked, standing between them. "Take a moment to get your shit together!"

Rob strained against Levi's hold, his face contorted in rage. "We're finished, man!" he snarled, his voice hoarse. "Two decades wasted!"

Carter wiped a streak of blood from his lip, his chest heaving. "You think I wanted this to happen?" he shouted, his voice cracking. "Bree didn't want to hurt you either. We didn't plan it, Rob—it just happened!"

"Shut the fuck up!" Rob roared, lunging again. Levi held him back with all his strength.

Tyler, standing off to the side, raised his hands. "Whoa, whoa. Everybody just take a break. This is a lot to take in."

Carter shook his head, muttering under his breath as he stepped back. "Fuck this," he said coldly. He turned toward the woods, grabbing his flashlight from the log. "You want to blame me for everything? Fine. Blame me. But I'm done."

"Where the hell are you going?" Levi called after him.

"Anywhere but here," Carter snapped, disappearing into

the darkness. The beam of his flashlight bobbed briefly before vanishing entirely.

The group stood in stunned silence.

Tyler ran a hand across the back of his neck, his expression grim. "You think we should go after him?" he asked hesitantly.

"No. Let him cool off," Levi said. "Everyone needs to calm down right now."

Rob sat slumped on the log, his head in his hands. The bracelet dangled loosely from his fingers, the firelight glinting off its stones. His shoulders trembled, though it was impossible to tell if it was from anger, heartbreak, or both.

Around them, the woods were creepily silent, as if the forest itself was stunned into stillness.

CHAPTER 15

The night had taken a sharp turn, its calm shattered and replaced by discord that gripped the group like a vice. What had started as an evening of camaraderie around the fire had shifted in an instant, leaving them stunned and reeling. The once-comforting warmth of the flames unable to cut through the cold shock settling over them.

Tyler broke the quiet first, his voice barely above a whisper. "Holy shit. I can't believe this has happened."

No one responded immediately. Rob sat slumped on the log, staring into the fire with a vacant expression. His jaw was clenched so tightly it looked like it might snap.

Tyson shifted uncomfortably in his seat, his fingers

drumming against the armrest of his chair. He exchanged a glance with Tyler, but neither seemed to know what to say. Levi, sitting beside Rob, leaned forward, elbows resting on his knees, trying to find the right words.

"Rob," Levi said softly, his voice measured. "I... I'm speechless, man. I didn't see that coming."

Rob laughed. "Yeah? Me neither."

Tyson leaned forward, his voice uncharacteristically serious. "Dude, I'm so sorry. This is... this is messed up."

"Messed up?" Rob snapped, his voice rising. "It's more than messed up, Tyson. It's...it's betrayal. From two people I trusted more than anything."

Tyson flinched slightly but didn't argue. Instead, he glanced toward Tyler, who gave a slow nod. "He's right," Tyler said. "It's the kind of shit you don't come back from."

Rob exhaled sharply, rubbing his temples with one hand while clutching the bracelet tightly in the other. "You know what's eating me up?" he said, his voice trembling. "I didn't see it. Not a single sign, no warnings... nothing. But the second I picked up this bracelet and realized it was Bree's—I knew. I knew exactly what it meant."

Levi hesitated before speaking. "Rob, people like Carter...

They're good at hiding things. And Bree... well, maybe she is too. You couldn't have known."

"Couldn't I?" Rob shot back, his eyes flashing. "We've been together for five years, Levi. How do you not notice something like this? How do you not feel it?"

Levi sat back, caught off guard by the question. He searched for an answer but found none. Tyson, ever the talker, finally spoke up again.

"Maybe she's just... I don't know, conflicted," Tyson said, though his voice lacked conviction. "Maybe she doesn't know what she wants."

Rob turned his gaze to Tyson, his expression hard. "Conflicted? Then why's she still planning the wedding, huh? Why go through with it if she's got... whatever this is with Carter?"

No one had an answer. The words hung heavily in the silence, unspoken but understood: Bree had made choices that none of them could justify.

"Maybe she's scared to blow it up. Scared of lookin' bad, scared of the fallout... who knows?" Tyler said desperately searching for answers.

Rob scoffed. "So instead of being honest, she just drags

me along? Lets me think we're building a future together while she's screwing my best friend behind my back?"

Levi leaned closer, his voice gentle but firm. "Rob, listen... this isn't your fault. None of it. This is on her. And Carter. They made those choices, not you."

Rob shook his head, his shoulders slumping further. "It doesn't make it hurt any less, Levi."

"I know, bud," Levi said softly. "I know it doesn't."

An uneasy stillness settled over the group, their energy drained as they searched for something—anything—they could say to offer Rob comfort. But no words came. Tyson absently poked at the fire with a stick, his usual liveliness absent. Tyler stood with his arms crossed, his gaze distant as he attempted to process everything that had unfolded.

"You're right, man," Tyler said after a while. "This is betrayal, plain and simple. Carter knew better. Bree... she knew better too."

"Yeah, well," Rob grumbled, his voice dripping with sarcasm, "knowing better doesn't seem to make a difference, does it?"

Levi placed a hand on Rob's shoulder, a gesture of quiet support. "You're allowed to be angry, Rob. You're allowed to feel whatever you're feeling right now. But don't let it tear you apart."

Rob didn't respond at first. He stared into the fire, his gaze centered on the bracelet he held. After a moment, he exhaled shakily and let it slip from his fingers, the delicate chain falling into his lap. "I just don't get it," he said, his voice nearly a whisper. "What did I do wrong? What wasn't enough?"

"Don't go there, man," Tyson said firmly. "This isn't about you not bein' enough. It's about them screwing up, not you."

Tyler nodded in agreement. "Yeah, Rob. Don't let their bullshit make you doubt yourself."

Rob rubbed his face with both hands, the betrayal almost too much to bear. He spoke softly, "I loved her." "I thought she loved me too."

The words landed with such force that no one could utter a sound, caught off guard by their impact. Levi felt a pang of sadness for his friend, knowing there was nothing he could say to truly make it better.

Tyson cleared his throat, breaking the tension. "Look... maybe this is just the universe's way of telling you somethin'.

Like, I don't know... maybe Bree wasn't the one."

Rob forced a laugh. "The universe can go screw itself."

The group chuckled softly, though the laughter was short-lived and laced with discomfort. They fell silent again, the awkwardness returning swiftly.

Just as the quiet began to feel suffocating, a sound broke through the stillness.

A piercing whoop echoed from deep within the woods. It was distant but loud enough to grab everyone's attention.

"What the hell was that?" Tyler asked, his voice sharp.

Before anyone could answer, another whoop came, this time from a different direction. Then another. The sounds overlapped, growing louder and closer, until it felt like they were coming from all directions.

Rob shot to his feet, the others following suit, their gazes darting to the impenetrable darkness beyond the firelight.

"Are those... animals?" Tyson asked, his voice strained.

"Animals don't sound like that," Levi said.

The whooping continued, rising and falling in an almost rhythmic pattern. It was unlike anything they'd ever heard—

deep and primal one moment, sharp, and ear-piercing the next. The sound carried an almost mocking quality, as if whatever was making it knew they were listening.

"Whatever it is," Tyler said, his voice shaking slightly, "it doesn't sound friendly."

They stood there, tense and still, as the surrounding forest seemed to come alive with noise. The whooping didn't stop, reverberating through the trees like a chorus of taunting voices.

"What do we do?" Tyson whispered.

Levi's eyes scanned the darkness. "We stay by the fire. Don't go anywhere. Don't split up."

The group instinctively huddled closer together, their earlier arguments and conflicts forgotten in the face of this new, unsettling threat. The crackle of the fire felt weak and insignificant against the overwhelming sounds closing in around them.

"Ain't no way I'm goin' anywhere," Tyson said, gripping a stick tighter as if it were a weapon. "Y'all can count me out of whatever hero plan you're thinkin' up."

"No one's going anywhere," Levi declared, his gaze fixed on the shifting shadows beyond the firelight.

And then, as abruptly as they had started, the whooping stopped.

The quiet that followed was deafening. The men stood motionless, barely daring to breathe, waiting for something—anything—to happen.

But nothing came.

CHAPTER 16

Carter trudged down the narrow trail, the beam of his flashlight swaying unsteadily as it cut through the dense shadows. His boots crunched against the dirt, the sound harsh against the faint rustle of leaves and the dim shimmer of the moon filtering through the canopy above. He was slightly drunk—more than slightly, if he was being honest—and the alcohol only made the chaos in his mind harder to ignore.

He shoved his free hand into his jacket pocket, muttering to himself. "Should've told him... should've ended it months ago."

Bree's words echoed in his head like a taunt. *It'll ruin everything. If you tell him, he'll never speak to you again.* She always had a way of keeping him quiet, twisting his guilt until it smothered him. He hated himself for listening, hated that he hadn't had the guts to come clean. Now it was all out in the open, and the damage was irreparable. Rob's devastated face was burned into his memory, and the thought of the others—his friends—seeing him as nothing more than a backstabbing scumbag made his stomach churn.

He kicked a loose rock off the trail, watching it vanish into the brush. "What the hell's wrong with me?" he said.

The flashlight wobbled in his grip as he focused on the uneven path ahead. Every step felt unstable, as if the ground itself mirrored his spiraling thoughts—a tangled mess of regret, guilt and anger that refused to quiet.

That's when he heard a faint sound, barely clear over his own steps—footsteps, matching his pace.

Carter stopped suddenly. The sound stopped too.

He held his breath, straining to listen. The forest remained silent, the quiet so complete it was almost deafening. Slowly, he exhaled and took another step forward. The crunch of his boot on the dirt trail echoed in the stillness.

Then came another crunch, this time not from his foot.

Carter's heart began to pound. "Tyson? Tyler? That you?"

His voice was shaky, barely loud enough to carry into the darkness.

No answer.

As he stood there, his nostrils flared at a sudden, overpowering stench so strong it made his stomach turn. His first thought was a skunk, but this smell was sharper, fouler, almost earthy, with an undercurrent of decay. He instinctively pulled his jacket collar over his nose and took a shallow breath, trying to block it out.

He swayed unsteadily on his feet, the alcohol dulling his balance. As he started walking again, the footsteps returned, perfectly mirroring his own. He stopped abruptly, his head snapping around as he swept the flashlight across the forest. Once again, the sound ceased.

"Alright guys," he called out, his voice firmer now, "now's not the time to mess with me."

The woods remained silent.

Carter swallowed hard, his pulse quickening. He turned towards the trail and started moving again, this time deliberately stomping his feet. The footsteps mimicked his every move, crunch for crunch. He felt a chill race up his spine as the realization dawned on him—this wasn't one of his friends.

He froze, clenching his fists. Slowly, he bent down and grabbed a large rock from the trail. "Whoever's out there," he said, his voice tinged with anger and fear, "this isn't funny."

With every ounce of strength he possessed, he hurled the rock into the brush. A dull *thump* echoed back, the sound of the rock striking something solid.

For a brief moment, there was nothing. Then, the rock came hurtling back out of the darkness and struck him square in the arm.

"Shit!" Carter stumbled back, clutching his arm as a sharp pain shot up to his shoulder. His chest heaved as he stared into the woods, his mind scrambling for an explanation. Animals didn't throw rocks. And his friends wouldn't mess with him like this—not after what had happened earlier.

Then it came—the growl.

Deep and menacing, it rippled through the air like a vibration from the earth itself. It wasn't just a sound—it was a force, curling around him, pressing against his chest, and sending a cold jolt through his core. It carried a raw, primal warning, unlike anything he'd ever heard, as if the forest itself had turned against him.

Carter's knees wobbled as he took a step back. "What the actual..." he whispered in disbelief, as his heart nearly pounded out of his chest.

Another growl followed, louder and closer. He just stood there, staring into the darkness, unable to move. Then instinct kicked in, and he turned, running blindly down the trail.

His boots thudded heavily on the dusty ground, each breath a strained gasp. The crashing sound of something huge moving through the brush behind him spurred him on. Whatever it was, it was fast, and it was getting closer.

Carter's eyes remained focused on the ground, the flashlight beam sweeping over the uneven trail, illuminating roots and rocks in its path. He glanced over his shoulder quickly, not sure what he would see.

Then, without warning, he slammed into something solid.

The impact sent him sprawling backward, landing hard on his butt. The air rushed out of his lungs as he clutched at the dirt, trying to sit up. Confused and disoriented, he looked up and instantly felt terror he had never known

Standing before him was something that shouldn't exist.

The creature loomed over him, its massive frame easily surpassing eight feet in height. Its shoulders spanned at least four feet across, giving it an impossibly broad and powerful appearance. Dark, coarse hair—about four inches long—covered its entire body, though patches around its face, chest and hands revealed leathery, weathered skin. Its oversized hands, disproportionately large even for its immense size, hung at its sides like tools of raw power.

The creature's head seemed to meld directly into its hulking shoulders, supported by enormous trapezius muscles. The top of its head tapered into a slight cone, giving it a distinctive and primal appearance.

The stench it carried was overpowering, a pungent mix of musk, decay and faeces that turned Carter's stomach. Its glowing amber eyes pierced through the darkness, locking onto Carter with a fiery intensity that sent a cold wave of terror through his entire body.

The beast's chest rumbled with a low growl, deeper than anything Carter had ever heard. It wasn't just a sound—it was a warning, a declaration of dominance. Its lips curled back, revealing sharp, glistening teeth that seemed made to tear flesh.

As he tried to move, Carter realized his body refused to obey. His legs felt like lead, his arms weak and useless. He could only stare as the creature loomed closer, its massive form eclipsing the faint moonlight above.

All Carter could manage to do was watch in horror as the beast stepped forward, its massive hand reaching out for him.

CHAPTER 17

Rob sat hunched on the log, staring blankly into the dying flames, his hands clasped tightly in front of him. The unopened bottle of whiskey lay beside Tyson, forgotten in the aftermath of the night's turmoil.

Levi sat across from him, his gaze flicking between the fire and his long time friend. Tyler and Tyson were both quiet, their usual banter absent as they shifted uncomfortably in their chairs. The unsettling events of the night lingered, leaving them on edge, and Carter's absence only amplified their anxiety.

Levi cleared his throat, breaking the silence. "Rob," he said softly, "you want a coffee or something? Might help take the edge off."

"Nah," he said as he kept his eyes on the fire. His voice sounded flat, devoid of the usual warmth that typically defined him.

Levi hesitated, unsure whether to press further. He wanted to say something—anything—to make Rob feel even a fraction better. But what could he say? What could anyone say after what had just happened?

"I still can't believe it," Tyler said finally, leaning forward in his chair. He rested his elbows on his knees, his fingers laced together. "Carter, of all people."

Tyson gave a quiet snort, shaking his head. "Man, I knew somethin' was up with him. Dude's been actin' weird all weekend. But I never thought..." His voice faded, and his jaw set in a grim line.

Rob ran his fingers through his hair, his frustration bubbling to the surface. "What pisses me off the most is that he didn't even try to tell me. Not once. He just sat there, pretending to be my friend, while he..." His voice cracked, and he looked away, swallowing hard.

"Yeah, it's shit all around, buddy," Levi replied as he shifted in his chair, his mind drifting to Carter. He'd been gone for over an hour now, and the anxiety feeling in his stomach was growing stronger.

"Should we... you know, go look for him?" Tyson asked, voicing the question that had been lingering in everyone's mind.

Rob didn't react, his gaze glued to the fire.

Tyler frowned, glancing toward the dark trail that Carter had taken. "I don't know, man. He stormed off pretty fast. Maybe he just needs time to cool off."

Tyson crossed his arms, his brow lowered. "He's been gone a long time. Like, over an hour. It's the middle of the night, and we're deep in the woods. What if somethin' happened?"

"Like what?" Tyler asked, his tone skeptical. "He's a grown-ass man. He can take care of himself."

"Yeah, but it's dark as hell out there," Tyson shot back. "What if he got lost? Or hurt?"

Levi rubbed his chest, the knot of anxiety tightening with every word. "I have to agree with Tyson on this one. No matter what he did, he's still our friend. And it's pretty damn cold out here away from the fire."

Rob finally stirred, sitting up straighter on the log. "You think we should go after him?" he asked, though his tone carried more reluctance than concern.

Tyson nodded. "We can't just leave him out there, man."

Rob sighed heavily, rubbing his face with both hands. "Honestly? I don't give a damn where he is right now." His voice sounded sharp, breaking through the tension. "But I don't want to sit here by myself, either."

Levi and Tyler exchanged a glance, neither of them surprised by Rob's admission. They knew his anger ran deep—it had every right to—but it wasn't safe to split up any more than they already had.

"Fair enough," Levi said. "Let's grab some flashlights and check the trail. Hopefully he is not far. If he doesn't want to come, we let him figure it out."

The others nodded, as they stood up. Tyler grabbed a flashlight from his tent, clicking it on to test the beam. "He's probably just sulkin' a little ways down," he said, though his voice lacked its usual confidence.

"Yeah," Tyson muttered. "Let's hope."

The group set off, their flashlights carving narrow beams into the thick darkness. Rob lagged slightly behind, his movements sluggish and stiff. It was obvious he didn't want to be out there searching for Carter, but the thought of staying alone in the dark, left with only his thoughts, was even worse. The unsettling whooping sounds from earlier lingered in his mind, amplifying the unnerving atmosphere that seemed to hang over the forest. Something about this place felt undeniably wrong.

As they walked, Tyler called out, "Carter! Hey, man, where you at?"

His voice echoed faintly amidst the trees, but there was no response. Levi shivered, pulling his jacket tighter against the cool night air. "Keep calling," he said. "He might not be far."

"Carter!" Tyson bellowed, his deep voice carrying farther than Tyler's. "Get your ass back here, man!"

Again, silence.

The trail stretched ahead, unnervingly quiet save for the rhythmic crunch of their boots on the dusty path. now and then, they stopped, listened, and called out Carter's name again. Each unanswered call added to the growing stress.

Rob finally spoke, his voice low and bitter. "Bet he's just sitting out there somewhere, feeling sorry for himself."

Levi glanced at him but didn't respond. He couldn't shake the uneasy feeling that something wasn't right. Carter might be a lot of things, but he wasn't reckless. He wouldn't just vanish like this.

Tyler stopped suddenly, swinging his flashlight in a slow arc across the trail. "You hear that?"

The others froze, their breaths catching in their throats as they listened intently.

"Never mind," Tyler said after a moment, dismissively shaking his head. "Thought I heard somethin'."

They pressed on, their calls for Carter growing more urgent as the minutes ticked by. Levi's worry deepened with every step, the silence around them now feeling unnatural.

CHAPTER 18

With each step, the four men struggled along the narrow trail, their flashlights flickering erratically through the thick trees. The frigid October air stung their cheeks, and the dead quiet of the woods unsettled them even more.

Levi and Rob had spent most of their lives in the woods but this, this felt very different.

Tyson, walking slightly ahead, suddenly stopped and crouched low, switching off his flashlight. "Yo, Tyler," he whispered loudly enough to make the others pause. "Did you hear that?"

Tyler, already on edge, swung his flashlight around, the beam slicing through the foliage. "Man, don't start with me.

What are you talkin' about?"

Tyson stayed low, his tone serious but with a playful edge. "I swear I heard somethin' movin' up ahead. Sounded like... I don't know, footsteps or somethin'. Big ones."

"Quit playin', Tyson," Tyler snapped, his voice tinged with nerves. "Ain't nobody out here but us. Stop actin' like a fool."

Tyson grinned in the darkness, suddenly standing up and flashing his light under his chin like a ghost story villain. "Or maybe it's Bigfoot comin' to snatch you up, bro!"

"Man, get outta here with that!" Tyler barked, swiping at Tyson's arm. His flashlight wobbled as he mumbled under his breath. "Ain't nobody scared of you. But I'm tellin' you right now, this ain't the time."

Levi sighed, his patience thinning. "Tyson, cut it out. We're not out here to mess around."

Tyson shrugged, still smirking. "Just tryin' to lighten the mood. Y'all look like you seen a ghost already."

"You're not helping," Tyler said, his voice tight. "And stop walkin' so far ahead. Nobody needs you wandering off."

Rob, trailing behind them, finally spoke up, his voice

sharp and angry. "Can we just keep moving? The sooner we find him, the sooner we can get the hell outta these weird ass woods."

The group continued walking, calling out for Carter every few steps.

"Carter! Yo, man, where you at?" Tyler called.

"Carter!" Tyson bellowed, his deep voice echoing. But the only response was the wind rustling through the leaves.

A few minutes later, Tyler broke the silence. "What do we do if we can't find him?" he asked quietly.

Levi's eyes flicked to him, his flashlight beam steady on the trail ahead. "Well, if we don't, we head back to camp and wait till morning. He'll probably come back when he's ready."

"And if he doesn't?" Tyler pressed.

Levi's jaw tightened. "Then we'll figure it out. But stumbling around in the dark all night isn't going to help anyone."

Rob laughed bitterly. "If he wants to sit out here and stew in his mess, let him. I don't care. But I'm not wasting my whole night looking for him."

Levi didn't respond. He couldn't ignore the feeling that the night was far from over.

They rounded a bend in the trail, and all four men stopped simultaneously. The air was thick with a foul, metallic odor, laced with a putrid undertone that made them want to vomit.

"Whoa, what the hell is that smell?" Tyler asked, pulling his jacket up over his nose.

Tyson coughed and turned away slightly. "Smells like somethin' died out here."

"That's blood," Levi said grimly

The others exchanged uneasy glances. Levi swept his flashlight around, the beam cutting through the foliage. At first, he didn't see anything. His light struck something, sending a shockwave through him.

"Holy shit!" Tyler shouted, stumbling back and nearly tripping. His flashlight wavered as he struggled to steady himself. "What... the fuck man!"

The others turned, and their collective gasps filled the air. High in the tree, about twelve feet above the ground, was Carter. His body hung limp, his head tilted at an unnatural angle. A jagged branch pierced straight through his chest, pinning him grotesquely to the trunk.

"Jesus Christ!" Tyler shouted, his voice cracking. "No! What is this?"

Rob stared, his face stricken, his hands clenched into trembling fists. "No. No, no, no. How... how did this happen? How is he up there?"

Tyson stepped forward slightly, his flashlight shaking as he pointed it higher. "This crazy man. Y'all think maybe... maybe he was climbing the tree and fell on the branch?"

"No way," Levi snapped, his voice harsh. "Look at him! The angle... the way he's skewered... That's not a fall, Tyson."

"Then how the hell did he get up there?" Tyson shot back, his voice shaking.

Tyler suddenly stepped away, his breathing quick and shallow. "This ain't right, man. This ain't right. We're out here, and Carter's up in a tree like that? What the fuck is out here with us?"

"Tyler," Levi said firmly, stepping closer to him. "Calm down. We're gonna figure this out."

"Figure it out?" Tyler's voice was shrill now, his panic escalating. "What are we even supposed to figure out? What could do that? Ain't no damn animal gonna do that! And if it's a person? Man, we're sittin' ducks out here!"

"Tyler, chill, bro!" Tyson barked, grabbing his brother by the shoulder. "Panickin' ain't gonna help. We stick together, all right? We'll get back to camp."

"And call for help," Tyler added quickly, as if grasping for hope.

Rob shook his head, his voice bitter. "We can't call. There's no damn signal out here, remember?"

Tyler's face fell, and his panic began to spiral again. "So what, we just wait for whatever did this to come for us next?"

"That's why we go back to camp now," Levi stated, his voice steady despite the knot in his stomach. "First thing in the morning, we come back with gear and figure out what to do. But right now, we need to leave."

As they turned back down the trail, the group instinctively bunched together, no one willing to take the rear. Tyson noticed and chuckled nervously. "Y'all fightin' to be in the middle, huh?"

"You think I'm walkin' at the back?" Tyler shot back. "Hell no."

"Not it," Rob said, stepping closer to the center. "Ain't no way."

Levi, leading from the front, kept his flashlight steady. "Just stay close. Nobody falls behind, all right?"

The banter was thin and forced, their fear barely contained. Tyler kept peering behind him, his flashlight flickering between the shadows.

"You hear that?" Tyler whispered, his voice tense.

"It's just us, man," Tyson replied, though his own flashlight was darting around the trees.

"Better stay just us," Tyler said.

As they hurried along, Levi couldn't get the image of Carter's body out of his head. It wasn't just the horror—it was the impossibility. Whatever had killed him was still out there, and the thought made his skin crawl.

"Keep moving," Levi insisted, his voice piercing the tension. "We're almost there."

Behind him, Rob mumbled, "This... this ain't right."

No one responded. They all knew it. Something sinister was out there with them.

CHAPTER 19

The group stumbled back into camp, their flashlights illuminating the clearing in erratic beams. The fire pit glowed faintly with the embers they'd left behind, the sight offering more than just light—it was a small anchor of comfort in the overwhelming darkness.

Tyler dropped his flashlight onto the nearest log and exhaled loudly, pacing near the fire as if trying to shake off the lingering terror that clung to him.

"Man," he said, "I could really use some of that fancy-ass whiskey you brought, Rob."

Rob, still ashen-faced and distant, didn't even look up. He waved a hand vaguely toward the bottle laying on the ground. "Go for it."

"You sure?" Tyler asked, hesitating for a moment.

Rob turned his eyes to him, his expression hollow and dark. "I found out my fiancée and my best friend are screwing behind my back, and then said best friend gets impaled on a tree branch 10 feet up. You think I care about a bottle of expensive booze right now?" He gave a bitter laugh. "Yeah, go for it. Hell, pour me some while you're at it."

Although startled by Rob's bluntness, Tyler quickly grabbed the bottle of whiskey and the knife from Carter's backpack. He popped the cap with a satisfying crack and poured some into a cup, the warm, smoky scent rising into the cool night air.

"Damn," Tyler said, sniffing the cup. "Smells fancy as hell. You sure your dad ain't gonna miss this, Rob?"

"He gave it to me," Rob said, gazing into the fire. "Figured I'd have something special for my bucks weekend. Turns out, I needed something to help me forget instead."

Tyler handed him a cup filled with the aged whiskey, and Rob took it without a word, draining it in one long gulp. Tyler raised an eyebrow. "Whoa, slow down, man. You trying to drown your sorrows already?"

Rob snorted and set the cup down beside him. "Considering the circumstances, a fine 12-year-old whiskey would be the perfect drink for a night like this."

Tyson grabbed a cup and poured himself some. "Damn," he said, taking a sip. "This is legit. Fancy and strong."

He handed the bottle to Levi, who shook his head. "I'll pass. Someone's gotta keep their head clear."

"Suit yourself," Tyson said, lifting his cup in mock toast. "Here's to survivin' the weirdest damn night of my life."

Rob gave a bitter laugh but didn't join the toast. Tyler glanced nervously at him and then back at the others. "Man, I don't even know what to say anymore."

"Don't say anything," Rob replied. "Just drink."

The alcohol provided temporary relief for Tyler and Tyson, but the underlying unease remained, a constant presence.

After a long pause, Tyson broke the silence again. "You know what's gettin' to me? We don't have anything to protect ourselves if whatever did that to Carter decides to come here."

Tyler lowered himself onto a log, his eyes darting toward the tree line. His voice came out quiet but tense. "Why did it... display him like that? Whoever—whatever—killed Carter didn't just leave him on the ground. It put him up in that tree. Why?"

Levi, seated near the fire, looked up quickly. He gestured toward the woods with the hatchet in his hand. "It wasn't just random. That was a warning."

Tyson frowned, gripping his cup. "A warning for what?"

Levi's expression darkened. "For us. It's saying we don't belong here. Well, at least that's my best guess."

Rob let out a bitter scoff, staring into the flames. "We got the message loud and clear."

Tyler shuddered, clutching the whiskey bottle tightly. "Man, this is some next-level horror shit. What kind of thing even does that? Not an animal. Not a human. So what the hell *is* it?"

The group fell into uneasy silence as Levi faced the fire. "We don't know what it is. It wants us to be scared, though. And we can't let it think it's working."

Tyson said, "Yeah, well it *is* workin'. This is some seriously creepy ass shit, bro."

Tyler lowered his cup and looked around. "You think it'll come for us?"

Tyson shrugged, his tone serious. "I don't know. But we saw what it did. And we got nothin'. No guns, no knives... hell, not even a stick sharp enough to fight back with."

Levi sat up straighter, his brow furrowed. "We have the hatchet."

"Hatchet?" Tyson snorted. "What you gonna do, chop down the thing before it eats you?"

"I don't know," Levi admitted. "But we've got to work with what we have."

"We should've brought a damn shotgun," Tyler said, with a dismissive shake of his head. "Next time I go campin', I'm bringin' a whole damn arsenal."

"Next time?" Tyson scoffed. "Man, there ain't gonna be a next time for me."

With his gaze fixed on the flames, Rob spoke with sudden sharpness. "What's the point of talking about weapons now? It's too late for that. We're out here with nothing, and Carter's dead. So unless one of you knows how to pull a rifle out of your ass, maybe we should focus on making it through the night."

Tyson glanced at the others as Levi rubbed his palms together, trying to think of something to say that might calm their moods. But before he could speak, a sound broke through the stillness.

A single owl hoot.

The group went still, instantly turning their heads toward the source of the sound. It came again—low and haunting, but mechanical.

"Those fuckin' owls again," Tyler whispered, his voice shaky.

"I don't think they're owls," Levi said, his eyes narrowing as he scanned the darkness beyond the firelight.

Another hoot reverberated through the woods. The sound was similar, but the ending warped slightly, finishing with an abrupt, off-key note.

"Nah, man, that's no ordinary owl," Tyson stated decisively, standing up. His gaze darted nervously, searching the darkness.

"What the fuck else is it then, bro?" Tyler asked, rising to his feet. His hand gripped the handle of the cup tightly, as if it might provide some protection.

Another hoot came, this time louder and closer. Then another, farther away. And another, to their left. The sounds were overlapping now, echoing among the trees in a disjointed, unsettling pattern.

Levi stood slowly, his heart pounding. "They're... surrounding us."

Rob, who had been silently seething, finally snapped. He stood abruptly, grabbed his empty cup, and hurled it into the woods with all his might. "Shut the fuck up!" he roared.

The group stared at him in shock as the cup was swallowed by the black abyss.

"Rob," Levi said cautiously, "I don't think—"

Before he could finish, the woods went deathly quiet. The hoots, the rustling—they all stopped.

For a short while, nothing happened. Then, with a sharp whoosh, the cup shot back out of the darkness. It just missed Tyler's head and struck a tent with a dull thud.

Levi turned to Rob, his face white. "Hate to say it, but... I told you so."

Tyler panicked. "What the fuck was that? What threw it back? Animals don't do that, man! They don't!"

Tyson grabbed his shoulder, trying to steady him. "Chill,

man. Panickin' won't help."

"Panickin'?" Tyler's voice cracked. "Somethin' just threw a cup back at us like it's playing fucking catch!"

Levi stepped closer to the fire, the hatchet in his hand. His voice was firm but low. "Everyone stay calm. If they wanted to attack us, they would've done it by now."

"Or maybe they're just waiting for the right moment," Rob mumbled darkly.

The forest seemed alive now, filled with faint creaks and subtle movements that kept them all on edge. Each man gripped their flashlight tightly, their eyes darting toward the tree line.

Levi stepped closer to the fire, speaking low but firm. "We don't know what they are or how many there might be, but there's four of us—four grown men. If we act fearful, if one of us breaks from the pack, that's when they'll strike. So let's just try to calm down and stick together."

Tyson let out a shaky breath, his gaze dropping to the ground. "You think that's enough?"

"It has to be," Levi said, locking eyes with him. "The fire and our composure are the best things we've got."

The group nodded reluctantly, their breathing still uneven, but Levi's words planted a fragile thread of resolve among them. They edged closer to the fire, its flickering light barely holding back the darkness as the forest seemed to watch and wait.

Another hoot echoed, louder this time, closer. Tyler backed away from the edge of the camp, his breathing shallow. "I don't like this. I don't fuckin' like this."

The sounds grew louder, sharper. Whatever was out there wasn't finished with them. It was waiting, toying with them, and the men could feel it drawing closer.

Tyler's eyes darted between the woods and the fire. "I know. We need torches. Thick logs we can light up—somethin' to keep these things back." He gestured toward the whiskey bottle he was clutching. "We soak the ends of the logs with this and set them on fire. Instant weapons."

Levi frowned, shaking his head. "In theory, sure. But you guys have been drinking, and the last thing we need is to set the whole damn forest on fire."

"Levi's right," Rob said, his voice firm but uneasy. "A torch isn't worth it if we burn ourselves out of here. We stick with the fire we've got."

Tyson, his face contorted in a scowl, gripped a thick branch like a club and said, "Great. We just sit here and wait for whatever this is to come get us?"

Levi glanced at the dark woods. "For now? Yeah. We stay put and keep that fire blazing. If it's the only thing keeping them back, we don't let it die."

CHAPTER 20

As the hours passed, the men drew closer to the warmth of the fire, the temperature steadily dropping. Levi poked at the fire with a stick, sending a shower of sparks into the air.

Tyson glanced toward the cooler. "Is there any beer left?" he asked quietly.

"The good stuff or the cheap stuff?" Tyler replied, reaching into the cooler.

"Cheap's fine, bro," Tyson said, shaking his head.

Tyler pulled out a can, cracked it open, and handed it to him. Tyson took it without a word, staring at the fire for a long moment before adding, "We should've never come to this place, man."

Tyler nodded, taking a swig of his own beer. "Yeah, somethin's just not right with this place," he said, his voice quieter than usual. "Maybe whatever was makin' those sounds is the same thing that killed that deer we saw yesterday." He paused, glancing toward the woods. "I can't wait to get the hell outta here tomorrow."

The men agreed. They couldn't wait for morning to arrive.

An hour passed without any sign of movement from the forest. The night remained quiet, almost too quiet, but the group stayed on edge, each lost in their thoughts.

Tyson, fighting exhaustion, dozed off where he sat, his head propped on his hand. When his hand slipped from his knee, he jolted awake, blinking in confusion as he glanced around.

"What was that?" he questioned, his voice groggy.

Levi chuckled softly, his tone dry but not unkind. "You woke yourself up, buddy."

Tyson rubbed his face, muttering something under his breath before shaking his head. "We can't stay up all night," he said finally, his voice heavy with fatigue. "We're dead on our feet. We have to sleep."

"Sleep?" Tyler's voice cracked, his eyes wide with disbelief. "You serious? After everythin' that has happened? Hell nah, man!"

Tyson sighed and leaned forward, elbows on his knees. "Man, we gonna need our strength if this mess keeps up. You think we can just sit here till the sun's up?"

"What if whatever's out there comes back while we're asleep?" Tyler shot back, his voice rising. "You think it's just gonna let us take a nap?"

Levi stepped in before the argument could escalate. "I'll stay up," he said firmly. "I wasn't planning on sleeping anyway."

Rob shifted beside him, his voice slurred from the whiskey. "I'll stay up too."

"You don't have to—" Levi started, but Rob cut him off.

"I want to," Rob said firmly. "I'm not ready to close my eyes yet."

Tyson glanced at the two of them, then at his brother. "Y'all can stay up if you want, but I'm not about to sit out here waitin' for somethin' to grab me. I'm gonna try to sleep."

Tyler gave Levi a tired look. "Yeah alright, I'm with him. Y'all wake us if anythin' happens."

Without another word, the brothers disappeared into the tent, Tyson's flashlight casting a brief beam of light before fading. The tent zipper slid shut, and within minutes, the sound of loud, rhythmic snoring filled the camp.

Levi and Rob exchanged a look, surprised at how quickly the brothers passed out. Rob shook his head and took another swig from his cup. The firelight caught the exhaustion and frustration etched into his face.

After a while, Rob spoke, his words slurring. "You know what the worst part is? My best friend is dead, and I can't even ask him why he did this. Why he... why he slept with her."

Levi glanced at him, his brow furrowed. "I'm sorry, Rob. I can't imagine how that feels."

Rob sighed heavily. "You know what else is eatin' at me? It's not just what they did. It's the question of how Carter even got her bracelet. Did she give it to him? How long was this goin' on? I trusted him. Hell, I trusted both of them."

Levi hesitated, unsure of what to say. "That's a lot to unpack, Rob. But maybe it doesn't matter how it started. What matters is you didn't deserve it."

Rob snorted, his voice edged with bitterness. "None of it matters now, does it? Carter's gone. And Bree... Bree's gonna have to answer for this when I get back. There's no way we're getting married now. We'll lose all the deposit money, probably have to sell the house. The list goes on."

Levi glanced briefly at the woods and back at Rob. "One step at a time, Rob. Let's just focus on getting out of here first."

Rob opened his mouth to respond, but something caught his eye. He stiffened, his gaze locked on the edge of the clearing. "Levi," he whispered hoarsely. "Do you see that?"

Levi turned his head sharply, his eyes widening. Just beyond the firelight, a shadow shifted—a tall, broad figure with glowing amber eyes, watching them from the tree line.

Briefly, neither man moved, frozen by the sheer impossibility of what they were seeing. The figure didn't move either, as if daring them to react.

"Wake the others," Levi whispered.

Rob nodded, his hands trembling as he crawled toward the tent. "Tyson. Tyler. Get up," he hissed, shaking the nearest sleeping bag. "Now."

The brothers groaned groggily, but the urgency in Rob's

voice snapped them to attention. "What is it?" Tyson asked, sitting up.

"There's somethin' big out there," Rob said with a shaking voice. "Right at the edge of the firelight."

As the brothers scrambled out of the tent, Levi kept his gaze fixed on the figure. But when they turned their flashlights toward it, the shape vanished into the night.

"What'd y'all see?" Tyson asked, his voice sharp with nerves.

Rob hesitated, glancing at Levi. Levi took a deep breath and said, "We saw a silhouette. It was massive—at least ten feet tall—and shaped like a human."

Tyler blinked, and scratched his head. "Wait. What if it's... ghosts or somethin'?"

Tyson smacked his brother lightly on the shoulder, his laugh strained. "Ghosts? How the hell ghosts throw things, you idiot?"

Before anyone could respond, a loud, crashing sound erupted from the woods. The noise was deafening, something large and heavy barreling through the underbrush, heading straight for the camp. The men all turned their attention to the sound, using their flashlights to try and see what was making the sound.

"Stay together!" Levi barked, gripping his hatchet tightly.

"What the actual fuck?" Tyson mumbled.

From the darkness, a massive, hulking shape charged toward them, stopping just shy of the firelight. Its form was shrouded in shadows, but its immense size was unmistakable—easily towering over any of them. A low, sinister growl rumbled from its chest, vibrating through the air and into their bones. The sound was so raw, so primal, that it rooted them in place, their instincts screaming to flee but their bodies refusing to move.

Except for Tyler. He broke from the group, bolting toward the tent, diving inside, and zipping it shut in one frantic motion. "Oh, hell no!" he yelled from within.

Before anyone else could react, the creature emitted a sharp grunt and hurled something—a rock—directly at the fire. The impact sent a spray of embers bursting into the air, a cascade of fiery sparks swirling chaotically around the group.

"Shit!" Levi cursed, throwing his arm up to shield his face as the glowing remnants rained down.

Rob slapped at his pants, brushing off the embers that

clung to the fabric. His wide eyes locked onto the dark silhouette just beyond the firelight. "This... this can't be real."

Tyson grabbed a thick log from the ground near the fire and hurled it toward the figure. "Back off!" he yelled, his voice shaking with both fear and defiance.

The log soared through the air, landing near the creature's feet. It stepped back into the darkness, letting out another deep growl before retreating into the woods. The crashing sounds of its departure echoed, leaving the men shaken and on high alert.

"What just happened?" Rob said, his voice still unsteady.

Levi scanned the darkness, his heart pounding. "I think it was testing us."

"Testin' us for what?" Tyson asked, his voice barely above a whisper.

Levi stared into the darkness and didn't answer. Whatever the creature was, it wasn't gone—it was waiting. Watching.

CHAPTER 21

Tyson stood near the tent, arms crossed, his flashlight aimed toward the zipper. "Tyler, come on, man. You can't stay in there all night."

"I ain't comin' out!" Tyler shouted from inside, his voice muffled but sharp with fear. "Y'all saw that thing, same as me. You think I wanna be next?"

"No, but we're all here together, bro. We gotta stick close. Now stop actin' like a bitch and get your ass out here."

There was a long pause. The only sound was the fire crackling. Finally, with an exaggerated groan, the zipper slid down, and Tyler poked his head out. "Y'all swear it's gone?"

"It's gone," Levi said firmly. "For now, at least. But we

need to keep the fire up and stay alert. So come out, sit down, and help us figure out what the hell's going on."

Reluctantly, Tyler climbed out of the tent, his head on a swivel. He shuffled to the fire, sitting close to Tyson and rubbing his arms as if trying to ward off the cold—and the fear. Rob sat on a log, staring into the flames with hollow eyes, while Levi crouched nearby, feeding another log into the fire.

"We need to build the fire back up," Levi said, his voice tense. "It threw that rock straight at the fire—clearly trying to put it out. If it succeeds, we'll be in total darkness... and as good as dead."

"I still can't believe this is happening," Rob said. He took a swig from the whiskey bottle, his hand trembling slightly. "That thing... it wasn't human. It wasn't an animal. What the hell was it?"

Tyson shifted uneasily, his eyes flitting in the direction of the trees. "Y'all saw it, right? That thing looked like... like a Bigfoot."

Tyler turned to him sharply, his eyebrows raised. "Wait a damn minute. You always said Bigfoot was a load of crap."

"No, I didn't," Tyson said, shaking his head. "I said most people's stories were a load of crap. But I always believed they might be out there. Hell, I think I saw one when I was a kid."

Tyler blinked in surprise. "You never told me that."

"Yeah, well, I wasn't gonna tell you when all you did was clown on me for believin' in stuff like that," Tyson shot back, a faint smirk tugging at his lips. "But I did. We was campin' with Dad, and I swear I saw somethin' big movin' between the trees. Thought it was a bear at first, but bears don't walk like that. Didn't say nothin', though, 'cause I knew nobody'd believe me."

Tyler stared at his brother, his expression shifting from disbelief to realization. "You serious?"

"Dead serious," Tyson replied. "And now? After tonight? You gonna tell me you don't think Bigfoot's out here? That it didn't kill Carter?"

Tyler shook his head slowly, his flashlight resting limply in his lap. "Man, I've been givin' you shit all these years, and now I don't know what to think. Maybe you was right."

Levi adjusted his grip on the hatchet. "I agree with Tyson," he said. "No doubt in my mind now—it was a Sasquatch. I didn't wanna believe it, but it couldn't have been anything else."

Tyler blinked, looking between them. "A what?"

"Sasquatch," Levi repeated. "It's the more traditional name for Bigfoot. Using 'Bigfoot' sounds goofy and there was *nothing* funny about that thing. Maybe how unrealistically huge it was, but other than that? That thing was a beast. And if it's out there, you can bet it's not alone."

Rob emitted a strained chuckle, shaking his head. "The weirdest night of my life just got weirder. Freakin' Sasquatch?" He sighed and mumbled, "Should've stayed home."

"Shit," Tyler said as he looked out into the dark woods. "I'd rather be anywhere but here right now."

"You and me both bro," Tyson replied.

 Rob passed the whiskey bottle around, the men taking sips one by one—except for Levi, who waved it off.

The bottle finally made its way back to Rob, who drained the last of it and set the empty bottle down with a hollow clink. "What do we do now?" he inquired, his voice "We just sit here and wait?"

"Wait for what?" Tyler snapped, his voice rising. "For big ass bigfoot to come back and finish us off?"

"Keep it together, Tyler," Levi said sharply.

Before Tyler could respond, a loud, sharp CRACK echoed through the forest, piercing the air like a gunshot. They scrambled to their feet, their heads snapping toward the sound. A second later, a massive tree came crashing down just beyond the edge of the firelight, its branches snapping and splintering as it hit the earth with a deafening thud.

"Holy shit!" Tyler yelled, jumping up and down.

"Stay calm!" Levi barked, though his own voice was tight with fear. He gripped the hatchet tightly, his eyes scanning the darkness.

"Calm?" Tyler's voice was almost a shriek. "A damn tree just fell, Levi! You think that's somethin' to be calm about?"

"It's tryin' to scare us," Tyson said, his voice steady. "That's all it is. It's just tryin' to mess with us."

"Well, it's workin'!" Tyler shouted, pacing near the fire. "What if it wasn't just tryin'? What if it comes back?"

"Tyler, stop!" Levi snapped. "You're not helpin' anybody by losin' it. Sit down and breathe."

But Tyler didn't sit. His hands shook as he paced, his flashlight beam jerking erratically across the ground. "We're all gonna die out here," he mumbled. "We're all gonna die."

"Tyler," Tyson said softly, stepping toward his brother. "Look at me. Just look at me, okay?"

Tyler stopped pacing, his eyes wide and glassy as they locked onto Tyson's. "What?" he whispered.

Tyson placed a hand on his shoulder. "We're not gonna die, aight? Not tonight. Not tomorrow. But you gotta calm down. We need you with us, man."

Tyler swallowed hard, his breathing shallow. "How you stay so calm?"

Tyson hesitated, then looked toward the fire. "I'm prayin', bro. That's all I got right now."

Tyler let out a hollow laugh. "You? You don't even go to church."

Tyson shrugged. "Don't need to go to church to pray. And right now? Now's the time, ain't it?"

Rob gave a sinister chuckle, shaking his head. "Prayin' ain't gonna stop that thing."

"Maybe not," Tyson said, his tone firm. "But it's keepin' me steady. You got somethin' better?"

Rob exhaled sharply, rolling his shoulders before standing up. "Yeah, I got somethin'," he said, swaying slightly as he rose. He grabbed the empty whiskey bottle near his feet, stumbled forward, and launched it into the woods with a surprising amount of force. "Take that, *Shitsquatch!*" he bellowed, his voice echoing in the dark.

He didn't stay upright long, falling hard onto his backside with a loud thud.

"Dammit, Rob!" Levi barked, spinning toward him. "Stuff like that's just gonna piss it off!" He gestured toward Tyler, who sat hunched and silent, fixated on the fire like he wasn't even there. "As if I don't have enough to deal with, I've gotta babysit a bunch of drunk men—one antagonizing a ten-foot beast and the other losin' the fucking plot."

Levi's voice rose to a shout, raw with frustration. "Get your shit together, guys!"

The men silently agreed, understanding that this was not the moment to exacerbate the problem.

CHAPTER 22

Rob exhaled slowly, tilting his head back to look at the sky. The whiskey's warmth buzzed through him, but it did little to dull the mental exhaustion weighing him down. His voice was low, just slurred enough to hint at his state. "How long till sunrise?" he asked, words dragging a bit, directed at no one in particular.

Tyson pulled out his phone and tapped the screen. "Four hours," he said, squinting at the faint glow. "Give or take."

"Four hours?" Tyler exclaimed, his voice cracking. "You serious? Feels like we been sittin' here forever."

"It's goin' to be a long four hours," Tyson said flatly.

The men exchanged nervous glances. They were all

exhausted, their nerves frayed from the relentless fear. Rob rubbed his temples, his movements slow and shaky, occasionally missing his mark and brushing his forehead instead. Tyler sat hunched over, biting his nails, while Tyson stared into the fire, its glow reflecting in his wide, glassy eyes.

Rob sighed heavily. "We can't keep this up," he said, his words wobbling just slightly, as if he were steadying his thoughts as much as his voice. "We're gonna lose it if we don't get some sleep."

Levi glanced at him sharply. "You think we're safe enough to sleep? I don't think that's a great idea."

"Come on, man, let's be realistic," Rob said, shaking his head slowly. "Whether we're out here or in the tent, we're in danger either way."

"I hate to say it, but Rob's right," Tyson said. "We're too damn tired and too damn tipsy. If somethin' comes back, we won't even have the energy to fight it off."

Levi frowned, his eyes scanning the tree line beyond the firelight. Every instinct screamed at him to stay awake, to keep watch, but the exhaustion on their faces was unmistakable. He felt it too. The others—especially after drinking—were nearing their breaking point.

"Fine," Levi said reluctantly. "But we don't spread out. Two to a tent."

"I'm with Levi," Rob said immediately. "I ain't sleepin' alone."

"You and me, bro," Tyler said, resting a hand on Tyson's shoulder. "No way I'm sleepin' in a tent alone after what we just saw."

The fire was stoked one last time, the flames casting flickering light over the camp as they reluctantly crawled into their tents.

Rob collapsed onto his sleeping bag with a heavy sigh, his breathing already slowing as he succumbed to the alcohol-fueled haze of exhaustion. Levi lay down beside him, not letting go of the hatchet in his hand. His body was stiff, his nerves on edge, while he attempted to calm himself down enough to sleep.

In the other tent, Tyson, and Tyler settled into their own uneasy rest. Tyson mumbled a complaint about Tyler being too close but they drifted off quickly, the adrenaline finally giving way to fatigue.

Levi, however, couldn't sleep. His mind played through everything that had happened—Carter's body, the growls, the screams and the massive silhouette that had loomed just beyond the firelight. Every time his eyelids grew heavy, he'd hear a sound in the forest, and his eyes would snap open again.

He wasn't sure how much time had passed when he finally started to drift off. His grip on the hatchet loosened, his breathing slowed, and his body sank deeper into the sleeping bag. The sounds of the night faded into the background, replaced by the dull hum of near-sleep.

Thud. Thud. Thud.

Levi's eyes shot open, his heart racing wildly. Footsteps. A faint but undeniable rhythm pulsed beneath their feet, originating from the edge of the camp. He felt his pulse quicken, every fiber of his being demanding stillness, as he strained to hear any sound.

The footsteps grew louder, closer, and then another set joined them, coming from the opposite direction. The rhythmic crunching surrounded the camp, circling like predators stalking their prey.

Levi drew in a sharp breath. *Not one... two. Shit.*

With his eyes shut tight, he held the hatchet in both hands. He was shaking, but his focus was singular. *Please go away, please go away,* he repeated silently, over and over, as if willing the creatures to leave them alone.

The footsteps stopped, and a hush fell over the camp. Then, one of the creatures began to approach his tent. Slowly, deliberately, its heavy footfalls shook the ground, each step closer than the last.

Levi's terror spiked as the steps stopped right beside him. He could feel the weight of its presence, the way the earth seemed to vibrate beneath it. Then came the sound that would haunt him forever: the deep, labored-breathing of something massive. The sound was wet and raspy, like a beast with enormous lung capacity, sucking in air through a chest the size of a barrel.

Levi's teeth clamped together in a silent struggle. He could hear the breathing just inches away, the thin fabric of the tent the only barrier between him and whatever was out there.

Please go away, please go away.

A deep, resonating growl, almost like a tremor, shook through Levi's chest. It was the kind of sound that made every primal instinct scream *danger.* Levi's eyes stung with tears he refused to shed, his lips moving silently as he repeated his mantra.

Then, mercifully, the growl stopped. He heard the creature straighten up, its massive frame shifting as it moved away. But it didn't leave the camp. Instead, it headed for the other tent.

Levi opened his eyes, his body stiff with terror, as the night was shattered by an ear-splitting scream. It was a sound unlike anything he had ever heard—shrill and piercing at first, then dropping into a guttural roar that seemed to shake the earth.

Inside the other tent, Tyson and Tyler jolted awake, clutching their ears as the sound assaulted them, relentless and deafening. Tyler's panicked screams and Tyson's frantic shouts were swallowed by the unholy noise.

In Levi and Rob's tent, both men clapped their hands over their ears, their faces twisted in agony as the sound seemed to tear through their skulls. And then, as abruptly as it had begun, the scream ceased.

The stillness that followed was almost worse than the sound itself. Their ears rang violently, a faint hum that dulled everything around them. They barely noticed the heavy footsteps retreating into the woods, the sound muffled by their damaged hearing. The vibrations of the creature's retreat faded before they could fully register it, leaving the camp wrapped in an eerie, disorienting silence.

Levi didn't wait. Gasping for breath, he stumbled out of the tent, his legs unsteady and made for the fire. The others followed quickly—Rob, bleary-eyed and shaky; Tyson, clutching Tyler's arm as his brother mumbled incoherently, his hands still over his ears.

They huddled near the fire, their faces pale and drawn. The ringing in their ears made the world feel distant, their own breathing unnaturally loud against the backdrop of fear.

Finally, Tyson broke the silence, his voice hoarse. "These things... they're not going to leave us alone, are they?"

No one answered. As they watched the flames dance, a chilling dread hung over them, heavy and inescapable.

CHAPTER 23

As he stared at the dwindling flames, the knot in Levi's stomach tightened. He knew what had to be done, but the thought of saying it aloud made his throat dry.

Finally, he spoke, his voice reluctant but firm. "We're gonna need more firewood."

The others turned to look at him, their faces dropping at the realization. Tyler immediately shook his head, his wide eyes betraying his panic. "Hell nah. I am not goin' out there with those things! Are you crazy?"

"Man, I'm with him," Tyson said, crossing his arms. "We ain't got enough light to see what's out there. You want us to walk right into one of 'em?"

Levi sighed, rubbing his temples. "Look, I don't want to go out there either. But if we don't act, the fire's gonna die, and then we'll be in complete darkness. You think that's safer?"

The group fell silent, wishing there was a better alternative. Staring into the flames, Rob replied. "Levi's right," he said reluctantly. "We can't let the fire go out."

Tyler threw up his hands. "So what? We just walk out there and hope they don't snatch us up one by one?"

"No," Levi said. "We stick together. All of us. We grab what we can as fast as we can and come back. But if we don't do this, we're sitting ducks."

Tyson gestured in exasperation. "This is insane."

"Nope," Levi said "It's survival."

After a brief pause, the men nodded reluctantly. Grabbing their flashlights—Tyler taking Carter's—they cautiously stepped away from the fire, the circle of light shrinking behind them.

The group crept along, their quiet footsteps the only sound that dared to break the silence.

"Man, I don't have good feelin' about this," Tyler said, his voice shaking. "Why does it have to be so damn quiet? Like, where's all the bugs and racoons and stuff?"

"It's unnatural," Rob said, glancing over his shoulder. "The whole place feels... off. I've been here plenty of times over the years, and it's never felt like this before."

"Creepy as hell, that's what it is," Tyler said, his flashlight beam trembling as he scanned the trees. "I swear, if somethin' jumps out, I'm gonna lose my—"

"Tyler, shut up," Tyson snapped. "You're not helpin'."

Levi crouched down, picking up a thick branch. He gestured to Tyson, who bent to grab another piece of wood. "We're almost done," Levi said quietly. "Just a little more."

The men continued gathering sticks, their flashlights bouncing erratically as they searched the ground. Tyler stood nearby, nervously glancing into the darkness. "I don't like this, man," he muttered. "I don't like this one bit."

"No one does," Rob said, shoving a handful of sticks under his arm. "Just keep it together."

Suddenly, a loud thump echoed among the trees, followed almost immediately by a second, duller thump.

Levi and Tyson straightened up immediately, their

flashlights darting toward the sound.

"What the hell was that?" Tyson asked, his voice tight with fear.

"Tyler?" Levi called, his heart pounding. "You see anything?"

There was no reply.

Tyson stepped closer, his flashlight sweeping toward his brother. His jaw dropped, and he stared in shock. When he finally spoke, his voice trembled. 'Oh my God... Tyler...

Levi turned his beam toward Tyler and staggered back. The side of Tyler's face was a mangled ruin, flesh torn away to reveal bone and muscle beneath. Blood streamed down his neck, glinting darkly in the flashlight beams. One eye was torn and bloodshot, its gaze unfocused and hazy, while the other stared wide and glassy, fixed in a blank, unseeing expression.

Tyler swayed on his feet for a moment, the flashlight falling from his limp hand. Then his knees buckled, and he fell to the ground with a sickening thud, collapsing in a heap.

Tyson emitted a strangled yell and dropped his firewood, rushing to his brother's side. "Tyler! Tyler!" he screamed, his voice cracking with panic. He grabbed Tyler's shoulders, shaking him frantically. "Say somethin'! Come on, man, say somethin'!"

Levi stumbled forward, his own flashlight trembling as he crouched beside Tyson. His stomach churned, bile rising in his throat as he took in the gruesome sight. "Tyson... stop," he said, his voice trembling. "He's—"

"No! He's still breathin'!" Tyson shouted, cutting him off. He knelt beside his brother, his hands shaking as he struggled to cradle Tyler's motionless body. "Help me get him back to camp! Now!"

Levi and Tyson carefully lifted Tyler, who released a gurgling breath. His limbs hung slack, his head lolling to one side as blood dripped onto the ground.

"Rob!" Levi yelled. "Grab the damn wood and let's go!"

Rob, his face ashen and his body shaking, nodded numbly as if in a daze. He scooped up the firewood and hurried after them, his flashlight swinging wildly in his hand.

They stumbled back into camp, the fire flickering weakly as they gently placed Tyler onto a sleeping bag. Tyson collapsed beside him, his face streaked with tears as he frantically checked his brother's breathing. "He's still alive," he sobbed. "He's still alive, but we gotta do somethin'! Levi, do somethin'!"

Levi's heart pounded, but he forced himself to stay focused. He crouched beside Tyler, his hands steady despite the chaos around him. The sight of Tyler's bloodied face was horrifying—half of it mangled, skin and muscle torn open. "We have to stop the bleeding," Levi said, his voice firm. He grabbed a shirt from a nearby pack and began tearing it into strips.

"Tyson, hold his head steady," Levi instructed. "Keep him as still as you can."

Tyson nodded, his hands trembling as he gently cradled Tyler's head. "Come on, Ty," he whispered, his voice breaking. "You can't leave me, bro."

Levi quickly tied the makeshift bandages around Tyler's head, pulling them snug to cover the worst of the wound. Blood soaked through almost immediately, but Levi adjusted and tightened the strips, muttering under his breath, "This has to hold. It has to."

"This can't be real," Rob said, his voice shaking as he stood near the fire, watching the scene unfold. "This is unbelievable. What hit him? A rock? How does something throw a rock that hard?"

"It was them," Tyson snarled, his glare piercing the shadows of the trees. "They did this. Those damn monsters are pure evil! Tyler did nothin' to them!"

Tyson's gaze shifted, his fury boiling over. He turned on Levi, his voice raw. "This was *your* idea! You're the one who said we needed more firewood! If we'd stayed here, this wouldn't have happened!"

Levi froze, his mouth opening and closing as he searched for words. Before he could respond, Rob stepped forward, his voice firm. "Stop it, Tyson. This isn't Levi's fault."

"Like hell it isn't!" Tyson yelled. "If he hadn't—"

"We had no choice!" Rob interrupted, his tone slicing through the chaos. "The fire was dying! We *had* to get firewood, or we'd be sitting in the dark, waiting to get picked off. You know that."

Tyson's jaw tightened, but he turned back to Tyler, his hands trembling as he tried to wipe blood from his brother's face. "We can't let him die," he whispered. "We can't. He's my brother."

Levi stood motionless for a short time, his heart pounding with guilt. He carried the burden of that decision, and now Tyler was hurt because of it. But the fire couldn't be allowed to dwindle—not now.

Taking a deep breath, he stepped forward, grabbed a few branches and logs, and carefully fed them to the flames. As the fire grew, its light seemed feeble against the haunting darkness surrounding the camp.

"We can't stay here," Rob said abruptly, his voice breaking the tension. "We can't. We gotta move."

"And go where?" Levi snapped. "We don't even know where they are. What if we walk right into a trap?"

Rob clenched his fists, his gaze darting to the surrounding trees. "Then what on earth do we do? Just sit here and wait to die?"

No one answered. The oppressive silence returned, broken only by the crackle of the fire and Tyler's ragged breaths.

CHAPTER 24

Tyson sat hunched near Tyler's sleeping bag, his flashlight clenched tightly in his hand. Tyler's shallow, uneven breaths were the only sound breaking the stillness. Every now and then, a faint, unnatural moan escaped Tyler's lips—a sound that worried Levi.

The subtle twitching of Tyler's fingers and the strange tilt of his head were signs Levi had seen before. *Brain trauma,* he thought grimly. His stomach flipped as a memory flashed in his mind—a school friend who'd died after a head injury during a football game. The twitching, the uneven breathing... it all came rushing back. He knew what it meant. It wasn't good.

He bit his tongue. Tyson didn't know. How could he? He

was clinging to hope with both hands, desperate to believe Tyler could pull through. Levi couldn't take that away from him. Not yet.

"You're gonna be fine, man," Tyson whispered, leaning close to his brother. "You've always been tough. Always." His voice trembled, but the determination in his tone was undeniable.

Rob sat a few feet away, gazing at the dim light of the fire. His face was drained of color, his eyes bloodshot from too much alcohol and the unbearable stress. "If they're out there," he said quietly, "why don't they just come for us already? What's the point of dragging this out?"

"They're messin' with us," Tyson snapped, his tone sharp. "They want us scared. They want us to break."

"Well, it's workin'," Rob admitted, his voice trembling. "Because I'm about ready to lose it."

Levi stopped pacing and turned to the others. "We can't afford to lose it," he said firmly. "If we do, we're dead."

Before anyone could respond, a sudden noise shattered the clearing—a distant snap of a branch, faint but deliberate. Levi instinctively grabbed the hatchet, his flashlight jerking toward the trees. Rob and Tyson jumped up to join him, their own beams cutting through the dense, foreboding tree line.

"They don't care they we can hear them." Rob whispered.

Levi nodded. "Stay close."

The snapping branches grew louder, accompanied by heavy, deliberate footfalls. The ground seemed to tremble with each step, sending faint vibrations through the dirt.

"They're comin'," Tyson said, his voice tight.

"Stay by Tyler," Levi ordered, his tone sharper than he intended. "Don't let them draw you away."

The noise intensified, a cacophony of crashing branches and rustling leaves echoing through the night. It came from all directions now, surrounding them. The men instinctively pressed closer together, their flashlights bouncing wildly as they tried to locate the source.

"Why are they makin' so much noise?" Rob said. "This isn't like before."

"They're tryin' to scare us," Levi said, gripping the hatchet tightly. "Keep your eyes open. Watch every angle."

The next sound was a series of deep, powerful growls echoing through the forest. One came from the left, another from the right, and a third from somewhere behind them. The sound was primal and menacing, almost unbearable.

"They're everywhere," Rob said, his voice trembling. "What do we do?"

"We hold our ground," Levi said, though his heart pounded in his chest. "Don't give them what they want."

The growling and crashing reached a terrifying crescendo, drowning out everything else. The men were so focused on the noise ahead that they didn't notice the silhouette moving silently through the woods behind them, slipping through the underbrush like a predator.

The Sasquatch crawled low to the ground, its massive form eerily spider-like as it moved on its fingertips and toes. Its long limbs stretched unnaturally, pulling its hulking body forward with an unsettling grace.

Tyson glanced back at his brother, his flashlight briefly landing on Tyler's still form. In that instant, everything seemed fine—Tyler lay motionless on the sleeping bag, his chest rising faintly with shallow breaths. Satisfied, Tyson turned his attention back to the crashing noises in the woods.

But then, the creature struck.

With terrifying speed, it lunged from the shadows of the trees, its long arms snapping out to grab Tyler by the legs. The unconscious man was yanked silently off the sleeping bag, dragged through the dirt, and swallowed by the darkness before anyone realized what was happening.

The crashing and growling stopped abruptly, plunging the camp into an unnerving silence. Tyson turned back toward Tyler's sleeping bag, his heart skipping a beat when he saw it empty.

"Tyler?" he called, his voice rising in panic.

Levi and Rob turned simultaneously, their flashlights darting to the empty sleeping bag. Levi's stomach dropped.

"Where is he?" Levi questioned, his voice strained.

Tyson scrambled toward the spot where his brother had been. "Tyler!" he hollered, his voice breaking. He frantically looked around and into the bushes. "Tyler!"

Levi's flashlight beam swept over the drag marks leading into the woods. His heart sank. "Oh, no..." he whispered.

Tyson followed Levi's light and saw the faint trail. His eyes widened, and a strangled cry escaped his lips. "No!" he screamed, bolting toward the tree line.

"Tyson, wait!" Levi yelled, grabbing his arm as Tyson gestured wildly toward the woods. "You can't just run out there!"

"They took him!" Tyson shouted, tears streaming down his face. He pointed toward the dark tree line, his hand trembling. "They took him, and we just let it happen!"

He ripped his arm free and landed on the ground, grabbing a handful of rocks. He hurled them into the woods with all his might. "Come on! You want a fight? Show yourselves, you fuckin' freaks!"

"Tyson, stop!" Rob yelled, stepping forward. "You're gonna get us all killed."

Tyson whirled around, his eyes blazing with anger. "Shut the fuck up!" he yelled, his voice raw. He grabbed another rock and hurled it into the trees. "You don't understand! That's my brother out there!"

Rob reached out, trying to pull him back. "Listen to me—"

Before he could finish, Tyson swung wildly, his fist connecting with Rob's jaw. Rob stumbled backward, nearly falling. "Damn it, Tyson!" he shouted, clutching his face.

Levi stepped between them, holding up his hands. "Enough!" he barked. "This isn't gonna bring Tyler back!"

Tyson stood with his hands on his hips, his chest heaving with anger and grief. "I should have protected him…" he whispered. "He's my brother…"

Rob rubbed his jaw, glaring at Tyson. "We all want him back," he said quietly. "But throwing punches isn't gonna help."

Tyson sank to his knees, tears streaming down his face. He dropped the remaining rocks and buried his face in his hands. "I couldn't save him," he choked out. "I couldn't save him…"

Before anyone could respond, an ear-splitting scream tore through the forest. It was high-pitched and piercing at first, like a woman wailing, before dropping into a roar that shook their bones.

"That's him," Tyson whispered, his voice barely a whisper. "That's Tyler."

"That's not him," Levi replied.

The scream was joined by another, equally horrifying, from a different direction. The two sounds overlapped, creating an unholy symphony that made the men's blood run cold.

Rob stumbled back toward the fire, his hands over his ears. "What do we do?" he shouted, his voice nearly drowned out by the noise. "What the hell do we do?"

Levi didn't answer. He stared into the darkness, his heart pounding, as the screams faded into a haunting silence. The forest seemed to hold its breath, waiting for the next move.

Tyson remained on his knees, his voice breaking as he whispered, "They took him... and I couldn't stop them..."

Levi crouched beside him, placing a hand on his shoulder. "This is not your fault," he said softly, though his own voice wavered. "I promise."

But as he stared into the endless black void of the woods, Levi couldn't shake the feeling that their time was running out.

CHAPTER 25

Rob sighed heavily, the sound breaking the quietness that had settled over the camp. He sat on a log, rubbing his jaw with one hand while staring into the faint embers of the fire. "What a damn night," he said, shaking his head.

Levi looked up from where he crouched by the fire, his eyes scanning the camp. His body ached from exhaustion, his thoughts a blur with everything that had happened. He glanced at Rob. "You okay?"

Rob winced slightly, rubbing his jaw again. "It's sore," he admitted, his voice flat. "But I'll live." He gave a weak, bitter chuckle. "Least of my worries right now."

Levi nodded, his gaze drifting to Tyson, who sat a few

feet away. Tyson was hunched over, his elbows on his knees, staring intently at the dirt. His flashlight lay forgotten beside him, and he hadn't spoken a word in what felt like hours.

Levi's stomach twisted. Tyson's silence was more unnerving than anything else. "Tyson," Levi called softly. There was no response.

Rob glanced at him, shaking his head slightly. *Don't push it,* his expression seemed to say.

Levi sighed quietly as he massaged the back of his neck. The cool air of dawn crept into the camp, and a faint glimmer of light began filtering through the dense trees. He stood, stretching his sore limbs, and glanced upward at the canopy, where the dark navy sky was softening into pale gray between the branches. "The sun's coming up," he said. "It'll be light soon."

Rob looked up, following Levi's gaze. "Finally," he mumbled.

Levi glanced at Tyson again, his voice firm. "Tyson, you hear me? We need to start getting ready."

Still, Tyson didn't move. Levi sighed again, louder this time, and took a few steps closer. "Tyson," he said, keeping his tone gentle but insistent. "It's time to pack up. Only take what we absolutely need—food, water, a flashlight. Leave everything else. We have to keep our packs as light as possible so we can move fast."

Finally, Tyson looked up, his eyes bloodshot and brimming with anger and grief. "I can't," he said, with a strained voice.

Levi frowned. "What do you mean, you can't?"

"I can't leave him," Tyson said, sitting up straight. His voice was firmer now, more resolute. "My brother's out there, Levi. I'm not leavin' without him."

"Tyson," Levi said, crouching in front of him. "We all want to find Tyler. But we can't stay out here. You saw what they did last night. If we don't leave, we're not gonna make it either."

"You don't get it," Tyson snapped, his voice escalating. "That's my brother. He's out there, scared, hurt—or worse— and you're tellin' me to just walk away?"

"I'm telling you we can't do anything for him if we're dead," Levi said, his own frustration surfacing. "If we stay here, those things will come back. They're not gonna stop."

"So what? We just abandon him?" Tyson yelled, standing abruptly. His fists were clenched at his sides, his whole body shaking with emotion. "You think I can live with that? Just go home like nothin' happened. What am I gonna tell our mother?"

"No one's saying that," Rob interjected, stepping forward cautiously. "But Levi's right. Unless we get out of here and get help, none of us are gonna make it back. You think Tyler would want you to die out here, too?"

Tyson turned on Rob, his anger boiling over. "Don't you dare tell me what my brother would want! You don't know him like I do!"

"Guys, stop," Levi said, stepping between them. He looked Tyson in the eye, his expression firm but empathetic. "No one's trying to tell you how to feel. But we're in over our heads. If we don't get out of here now, we're not gonna survive."

Tyson shook his head, his jaw rigid. "You don't get it," he said again, his voice cracking. "You don't know what it's like to lose a brother like this."

"I am so sorry buddy," Levi said, his tone softening. "You did everything you could."

"It wasn't enough," Tyson whispered, his shoulders slumping. He dropped back onto the log, burying his face in his hands. "It wasn't enough..."

Levi crouched beside him again, placing a hand on his shoulder. "We're not giving up on Tyler," he said quietly. "But staying here isn't gonna help him—or us. We'll go back to town, get more people, get supplies. We'll come back with what we need to find him. Together."

Tyson didn't respond right away. He sat in silence, his hands covering his face as he fought to steady his breathing. Finally, he lowered them, staring at the ground. "If we leave," he said slowly, "you promise we'll come back? You swear it?"

Levi nodded firmly. "I swear."

Rob chimed in, his voice steadier now. "We're not leaving him behind, Tyson. We'll come back."

Tyson took a shaky breath, nodding reluctantly. "Okay," he said finally. "Okay. But if we don't come back…" His voice trailed off, leaving the implication hanging in the air.

"We'll come back," Levi repeated, his tone resolute.

The men began gathering their gear, working quietly. Levi packed the remaining supplies, pulling out only the essentials. "Leave anything you don't need," he reminded them. "No extra weight."

Rob extinguished the remaining fire, kicking dirt over the glowing embers. Gathering Tyler's belongings, Tyson stuffed them into his backpack and stood looking at the place where his brother had vanished.

As the first light of dawn filtered through the trees, they felt a slight sense of relief.

"We ready?" Levi asked, slinging his pack over his shoulder.

Rob nodded. "Yeah. Let's get the hell out of here."

Though he didn't answer, Tyson stood and readjusted his pack, his expression somber. The three men exchanged a glance, their exhaustion, and fear mirrored in each other's faces.

The promise to Tyson burdened Levi as he started the trail. He didn't know if they'd find Tyler—or if they'd even make it back themselves. But he would do everything he could to escape the unforgiving forest and find his way back to safety.

CHAPTER 26

Rob's footsteps thudded heavily against the dirt trail, his breath quick and uneven. "We gotta keep moving," he said sharply, his voice breaking through the early morning. "We can't stop."

The three men were nearly jogging, their packs jostling with each hurried step. No one wanted to be at the back, and Tyson stayed close to Rob, his head swiveling as he glanced nervously at the trees. The soft light of dawn filtered through the canopy, but the forest still felt ominous.

The trail twisted and turned, the thick underbrush encroaching on either side. The cold air bit at their faces, and their breaths came out in misty puffs. None of them spoke for a while, the anxiety building with every step.

Levi stopped abruptly, causing Tyson to stumble to a halt behind him. "What the fuck..." Rob said, looking ahead. His voice was unsteady, his face ghostly white.

Up ahead, the trail was completely blocked. Three massive trees, their trunks thick and gnarled, were stacked deliberately across the path. The jagged ends of the trunks glistened with fresh sap, and splinters of wood littered the ground.

"Jesus," Levi breathed, stepping closer. His hand brushed against the rough bark as he inspected the barricade. "This isn't an accident. They did this."

Rob exhaled sharply, running a hand through his hair. "Can you even imagine the strength it would take to pull up trees like this? And to carry them—stack them—like it's nothing?" He gestured at the massive trunks. "That's not human strength. Not even close."

Tyson's eyes darted between the trees, his jaw tightening. "And it's not just strength. They're smart. This is a trap. They want us stuck here."

Levi nodded grimly. "Yep. I'd say so."

Tyson threw his hands up, his breathing quickening. "We're never gettin' outta here!" he yelled, pacing in frantic circles. "They're playin' with us, man! First Tyler, now this?

What's next?"

"Tyson, calm down," Levi said firmly, stepping toward him. "We'll figure it out."

"Figure what out?" Rob snapped, his voice loud and panicked. "They're picking us off! One by one! You think they're just gonna let us walk outta here? Who's next, huh? Me? You? Tyson?"

Tyson's pacing became more erratic, his movements jerky. "This is it, man!" he shouted, his voice strained. "We're done! We're done!"

Levi turned away from the argument, his eyes drifting over the dense trees behind them. Suddenly, a chill ran through him as he felt the blood drain from his body.

Emerging silently from the brush and onto the trail, less than ten feet away, was the massive figure of a Sasquatch.

It was enormous—easily ten and a half feet tall, its broad shoulders dwarfing the surrounding trees. Its hair was thick and auburn-colored, its deep-set eyes locked onto the group with an unsettling intensity. Its chest rose and fell slowly, the sound of its breathing clearly audible in the stillness.

Levi was shocked, his mouth dry with fear. His voice caught in his throat as he struggled to warn the others.

Rob noticed Levi's wide-eyed stare and turned to look. He drew in a sharp breath, his body rigid as he stared at the creature. "Oh my God..." he whispered.

"What y'all lookin' at?" Tyson asked, his brow furrowed as he turned to follow their gaze.

The second Tyson laid eyes on the Sasquatch, his mouth dropped. "Aw, hell no..." he said, his voice trembling.

The Sasquatch tilted its head slightly, its expression almost curious. Then its face twisted into an unsettling, sinister smile. It stepped forward, its massive foot landing with a heavy thud.

"Run!" Rob yelled, but before anyone could move, the creature lunged. Its long arm shot out, its clawed hand wrapping around Tyson's neck with terrifying speed.

Tyson gasped, his hands clawing at the creature's grip. "Get off....me!" he choked out, his voice strangled.

The Sasquatch's grip tightened, and with a sickening crack, Tyson's neck snapped. His body went limp instantly, his head lolling to one side.

"Tyson!" Rob screamed, his voice raw with desperation.

With effortless strength, the Sasquatch hoisted Tyson

over its shoulder as if he weighed nothing. Turning swiftly, it disappeared into the dense undergrowth. Its heavy footfalls faded quickly, leaving the trail unnervingly silent once again.

Rob dropped to his knees, his entire body trembling. He gripped his head with his hands as he shook uncontrollably, his breaths coming out in short, labored gasps. "This isn't real," he muttered. "This can't be real..."

"Rob, look at me," Levi said, crouching beside him. His own heart pounded with the shock and horror of Tyson's death, but he knew falling apart wasn't an option. They had to keep it together if they wanted to make it out of the forest alive. "You need to get it together."

Rob didn't respond. His shaking grew worse, his hands pulling at his hair as his breaths turned to sobs. "They're gonna kill us," he whimpered. "They're gonna kill all of us..."

"Rob!" Levi barked, grabbing him by the shoulders and giving him a firm shake. "We're still alive. We can still get out of this, but I need you to hold it together. Do you hear me? I need you."

Rob looked up at Levi, his eyes wide and tear-filled. He nodded shakily, though his breaths were still uneven.

Levi gave his shoulder a reassuring squeeze. "We have to keep moving," he said quietly. "Tyson's gone. We can't help him now."

Rob's face twisted in anguish, but he nodded again. "Okay…" he whispered. "Okay…"

Levi stood, gripping his hatchet tightly. "We can't get past these trees," he said, motioning to the barricade. "I saw an opening a little ways back. We'll go around, pick up the trail again."

Rob didn't respond, but he stood slowly, his hands trembling as he adjusted his pack. The two men turned and began moving quickly, their footsteps quick along the dirt trail.

Levi realized the rising sun brought no comfort now; its light did little to deter the Sasquatch. It would attack regardless. His gaze stayed fixed on the trees as he fought to focus on the path ahead, every nerve on edge.

Rob broke the silence, his voice hoarse. "Where do you think it took Tyson?"

Levi shook his head, his expression grim. "I don't know," he said quietly, glancing at Rob. "Best not to think about that right now, bud."

A few minutes later, they came across a break in the brush. Without a word, they veered off the trail, pushing through the thick undergrowth to find a way around the barricade the Sasquatch had built.

CHAPTER 27

Rob exhaled sharply, his breath visible in the crisp morning air. He rubbed his hands together as they trudged through the forest, the cold seeping into their bones despite their brisk pace. "How much longer do you think?" he asked, his voice breaking the quiet.

Levi didn't answer immediately, his focus on scanning the underbrush ahead. He kept his hatchet ready, the muscles in his arm tensed. "Not sure," he finally said. "Could be 3 to 4 hours depending upon how far off trail we end up."

The two moved quickly, their boots crunching over the dew-covered grass. They stuck close to each other, their senses on high alert.

Levi suddenly stopped in his tracks, holding up a hand

for Rob to halt. His head tilted slightly while he peered deep into the foliage ahead.

"What is it?" Rob whispered, his voice tight with stress.

Before Levi could answer, a blur of motion erupted from the brush. A deer burst out, its slender body bounding across their path in a frantic sprint. Its hooves scattered leaves and dirt as it ran towards a cluster of trees.

Levi let out a breath. "It's just a deer," he said, trying to slow his pulse.

"Yeah," Rob replied, his gaze lingering where the deer had come from. "But it looked like it was running from something."

Levi followed his friend's line of sight, his unease deepening. "Maybe a bear," he said, though his tone wasn't convincing. "Whatever it is, it's not just us and them out here."

"'Them,'" Rob repeated. "You mean the Sasquatch?"

"Yeah."

Their pace quickened as they pressed on, both keeping a close eye on their surroundings.

Rob glanced at Levi. "Do you think there's more out

there? Besides Sasquatch, I mean. Like other creatures we don't know about?"

Levi shrugged, his eyes scanning the trees as they moved. "Probably. The world's a big place. People haven't explored everything."

Rob laughed nervously, the sound hollow. "Great. Just what I needed to hear."

Levi allowed himself a small smile, though it didn't reach his eyes. "Focus on one nightmare at a time."

Rob chuckled faintly, but his gaze stayed sharp, sweeping the forest as they pushed forward. They were both terrified, both exhausted, but they were still moving. Still fighting. And that was all they could do.

As Levi stepped carefully over a fallen branch, he glanced at Rob. "Have you noticed?" he said quietly, his voice low. "The forest feels... lighter now."

Rob looked at him, his brow furrowed. "Lighter how?"

"Last night, when they were close, it was dead silent," Levi explained. "When there's a predator around, most of the time everything—birds, animals, even insects—go quiet. It's like the whole forest knows to shut up."

Rob nodded slowly, his face red from the cool morning air. "So, you're saying they're not nearby? Not right now?"

"Obviously I don't know for sure but it is a good sign," Levi replied, his voice carrying a hint of hope.

That small reassurance was enough to keep them moving. The dense underbrush clawed at their clothes as they pressed forward, but Levi set a determined pace. Rob stayed close behind, his nerves still raw and frayed.

They didn't speak much after that. The events of the past twenty-four hours loomed over them like a heavy cloud, each step a battle to push the haunting memories to the back of their minds.

After what felt like an hour of weaving through the dense forest, Levi slowed his pace, his eyes narrowing as he stared ahead.

Rob noticed and whispered, "What's up?"

Levi mumbled, "Keep moving, but look up on that far ridge."

Rob followed Levi's gaze and gasped. There, on a distant ridge, stood three figures silhouetted against the morning light. Two were massive, their broad shoulders and elongated limbs unmistakable. The third, smaller but no less intimidating, stood slightly behind them. They were still as statues, their attention clearly fixed on the two men below.

"Oh, shit," Rob breathed heavily. "They're just standing there. Watching."

Levi's anxiety grew. "Yeah," he said grimly, "and they want us to see them."

"What the hell are they waiting for?" Rob asked, his voice trembling.

Levi's jaw clenched. "Doesn't matter. Just keep walking."

Rob hesitated. "We don't have to go that way, do we?"

"No," Levi said quickly. "We'll keep low, circle around. Don't run. Don't panic."

The two men continued forward, veering slightly to avoid heading directly toward the ridge. But their eyes flicked nervously to the figures as they trudged along.

"They're coming," Rob hissed suddenly, his voice rising in panic. "Levi, they're coming!"

Levi turned his head and felt his stomach drop. The two larger figures had broken away from the smaller one and were now charging down the ridge at an unbelievable speed.

Their massive strides devoured the distance between them and the men, their movements smooth and predatory.

"Oh my God," Rob shouted, his voice cracking. "They're coming for us."

"Run!" Levi shouted, grabbing Rob's arm and yanking him forward.

They bolted, the underbrush whipping at their legs and arms as they sprinted. Branches lashed at their faces, cutting their skin, but the pain barely registered.

"Don't stop!" Levi yelled, his voice strained. "Keep moving!"

Rob tripped but caught himself, gasping for air as he fought to keep pace. The creatures were closing in, their immense strength and speed making it impossible to escape. The Sasquatch's crashing through the forest was deafening—heavy footfalls, snapping branches, and guttural growls that seemed to vibrate in their chests.

"They're gaining on us!" Rob cried, panic making his voice shrill.

"Shut up and run!" Levi snapped, though the fear in his own voice was undeniable.

Without warning, the forest opened up. Levi skidded to a halt, his boots sliding on loose dirt as he threw an arm out to stop Rob.

"Damn! That was close," Rob gasped, staring at the edge of a shallow ravine.

"We can't stop!" he panted, clutching his knees as he tried to catch his breath.

Levi didn't answer immediately. He stared at the rocky slope before them. It wasn't a sheer drop, but the descent was steep enough to be dangerous. Jagged rocks jutted out along the incline, and the ground below seemed unnervingly far for their rushed escape.

Rob straightened up, realization dawning. "You've gotta be kidding me," he said. "We can't climb down that."

"We don't have a choice," Levi said firmly. "They're still coming. Either we climb, or we're dead."

Rob hesitated, glancing nervously behind him. "I don't see them."

"That doesn't mean they're not there," Levi snapped. "Move!"

Levi dropped to his knees and gripped the rocky edge, his

hands trembling slightly. Rob followed suit, his movements clumsy but desperate. Together, they began their descent. Loose dirt and jagged stones shifted under their weight, cutting into their palms and scraping their knees, but they ignored the pain.

Levi glanced up briefly, scanning the ridge. The Sasquatch were nowhere in sight, but that only made the situation more unsettling. They could be circling, waiting for another chance to strike.

"They're out there," Levi mumbling to himself, his jaw tight. "They're watching."

Rob didn't respond. His focus was entirely on the climb, his breath coming in short, sharp gasps as he fought to keep his footing. The ground below felt impossibly far away, the safety it promised nothing more than a fleeting hope.

As they neared the bottom of the cliff, Rob finally spoke, his voice shaking. "What if they're waiting for us down there?"

Levi didn't answer immediately, his eyes scanning the forest below. "Then we keep moving," he said, his voice flat. "We don't stop."

Rob exhaled shakily, his hands gripping the rocks tighter. "This is insane."

"It is," Levi agreed. "But we don't have another option."

The last few feet of the descent were the hardest, the rocks slick with moss. Levi dropped to the ground with a grunt, his knees buckling slightly from the impact. He looked up to see Rob struggling with the final stretch, his face drenched in sweat.

"You're almost there, bud," Levi said, holding out a hand. Rob grabbed it, and Levi helped him down the last few feet.

They stood in silence for a moment, their breaths heavy. The surrounding forest was still, but neither man felt safe.

"We keep moving," Levi said quietly.

Rob nodded, though his hands still trembled. "Let's go."

Without another word, the two men started moving, their pace quick and determined. The nightmare wasn't over—not yet.

CHAPTER 28

The forest seemed endless, a suffocating maze of shadows and towering trees. Levi and Rob pushed through the dense undergrowth, their breaths sharp and uneven. Every muscle in their bodies screamed for rest, but fear drove them forward. Their sweat soaked through their clothes, making the fabric cling to their skin, mixing with the metallic tang of exertion and the earthy scent of pine.

"We're getting close," Levi called over his shoulder, though he had no idea where "close" might be. Safety? Escape? It felt like a lie, but he hoped it would spur Rob on.

Behind him, Rob stumbled, his boot catching on a root. "Close to what?" he said. "Dropping dead?"

Levi didn't answer. "Just keep moving, bud!" The sharp edge in his voice mirrored his own desperation.

Then the noise began. A sound ripped through the forest, sharp and unnatural, like a warped whistle or the scream of an animal in pain. It echoed among the trees, rising and falling in pitch, each call overlapping the next, building into a sinister chorus.

Rob's head snapped toward the sound. "Shit! Can't they just leave us alone!"

Another cry answered, this one farther to the left, high-pitched and grating. The calls multiplied, each one more jarring, until the woods came alive with a cacophony of whoops and shrill cries.

"Don't slow down," Levi shouted. The sounds seemed to bounce erratically off the trees, making it impossible to pinpoint their origin.

Rob's pace faltered. "My lungs feel like they are on fire!"

Levi's pulse hammered in his ears. "Don't stop, I said!" he shouted, forcing himself to focus on the path ahead.

The forest loomed tighter around them, the canopy overhead blotting out the sunlight. The whooping grew louder, now accompanied by the relentless crashing of heavy footfalls through the brush. It wasn't just noise—it was pursuit.

Levi looked back and saw Rob struggling to keep up, his face red and streaked with blood and dirt. His movements were clumsy, his exhaustion obvious.

"I can't keep going like this," Rob wheezed, his words broken by shallow breaths.

"Yes, you can!" Levi barked. His own legs felt like lead, but he pushed harder, forcing himself to override the burning in his muscles. His heart slammed against his ribs, matching the frantic rhythm of their escape.

Levi had never felt exhaustion like this before. He was drained, both mentally and physically, but sheer willpower forced him to keep moving.

The forest floor grew more treacherous, with roots and loose stones threatening to trip them at every step. Levi kept his eyes forward, weaving through the obstacles as best he could. But Rob was slowing down, the gap between them widening.

Then Rob's foot caught on something—a thick vine or root hidden beneath the leaf litter. He pitched forward with a startled cry, hitting the ground hard.

Levi didn't notice immediately, too focused on the sounds around them. It wasn't until Rob's voice tore through the air like a blade.

"Levi!" Rob screamed, raw panic in his tone. "Help me!"

Levi's momentum faltered as he turned, his eyes locking on Rob, who was tangled in the undergrowth. Relief flickered in his chest—Rob wasn't hurt, just stuck. But the feeling was fleeting.

The brush behind Rob exploded with movement, and an enormous figure barreled out of the shadows. Levi's breath stuttered as his brain struggled to make sense of what he was seeing.

The creature was ridiculously large, its chestnut-colored hair glinting faintly in the fractured sunlight. Its speed was unnervingly fast, each stride covering the distance in the blink of an eye. In an instant, it was on Rob.

"No!" Levi shouted, his voice cracking as he lunged forward.

Rob barely had a moment to react before the Sasquatch's massive hand seized him with brutal force. In one swift motion, it ripped him from the vines and hoisted him into the air as though he weighed nothing. His scream choked off abruptly as the creature slung him over its shoulder with effortless precision.

Levi stopped mid-step, his body locking up as the sheer horror of what had just happened overwhelmed him. His gaze met Rob's for a brief, searing moment. In that instant, he saw everything—the terror, the helplessness, the silent plea for salvation. But Levi stood still, his mind spinning with utter disbelief.

The Sasquatch vanished into the dense forest, its towering frame blending seamlessly with the shifting patterns of morning light filtering through the foliage. Rob's cries lingered for a fleeting moment before fading, drowned out by the rapid, haunting whoops of the others—a chilling chorus that sounded almost celebratory.

Levi stood there, rooted in place, unable to move as if the forest itself had closed its grip around him. His limbs felt like stone, his chest constricted with the crushing grip of helplessness. All he could hear was the pounding of his heartbeat and the ghost of Rob's last scream.

Then, out of nowhere, a voice thundered in his head, cutting through the paralysis like a blade.

Move!

The word slammed into him with the force of a gunshot,

jolting his body into action. He stumbled backward, then turned sharply on his heels and ran. His legs screamed in protest, but he forced himself to keep moving, desperate to escape the nightmare. The voice reverberated in his thoughts, pushing him forward with every step.

CHAPTER 29

Levi's chest heaved with every breath, and the sharp taste of bile rose in his throat. He barely made it to a tree before doubling over, retching violently. His stomach was empty, but his body still convulsed as if trying to expel the fear and grief tearing at him from the inside.

When the dry heaving subsided, Levi leaned against the tree, his forehead pressed to the rough bark. Tears stung his eyes, but he refused to let them fall. Not now. Not here. *"Keep it together,"* he whispered to himself, his voice hoarse and trembling. *"Just... keep moving."*

But his body betrayed him. Exhaustion dragged at his limbs, and every muscle screamed for rest. His mind was clouded with panic and grief—Rob's terrified face as the Sasquatch carried him away replayed on an endless loop in his thoughts.

Levi sank to his knees, rubbing his eyes. The trailhead felt like a distant memory, a mirage just out of reach. By now, he should have been out of these woods. The forest around him felt alive, watching, waiting. The sound of the whooping earlier still echoed in his ears, a reminder that he wasn't alone out here.

Levi glanced at the sky through the canopy. The sun was dipping lower, the light growing dimmer by the minute. He had maybe a few hours of sunlight left. And Levi knew that darkness was their time.

"I can't be out in the open," Levi whispered to himself, forcing his legs to move again. He stood up and stumbled forward. *"I need to find somewhere. Anywhere."*

His eyes darted around the forest, scanning for potential hiding spots. Trees were out of the question—with their oversized hands, powerful legs and long arms, the Sasquatch could climb effortlessly. Trying to hide in the branches would be futile. He needed something low, something hidden, something they wouldn't expect.

A hollow log caught Levi's eye, nestled between two towering trees and partially hidden by moss and ferns. He hesitated, weighing his options. It wasn't ideal—far from it—

but it was better than nothing. If he curled up tightly, he could squeeze inside, and the thick bark might provide some measure of protection. At the very least, it would conceal him, giving him a chance to catch his breath out of sight.

Levi crouched next to the log, inspecting it carefully. It smelled of damp earth and decay, but it seemed solid enough. He ran his hand along the inside, wincing at the rough texture. It was the best he could manage under the circumstances.

A sudden realization made him shiver. What if they could smell him? What if the creatures were already tracking him, their keen senses locking onto his scent? He needed to mask it somehow.

Levi grabbed his water bottle, pouring some onto the dirt. He worked quickly, scooping up handfuls of mud and smearing it across his arms, legs and face. The cold, wet earth clung to his skin, seeping into the cuts and scrapes that burned with every touch. He shuddered at the sensation, the sting making him wince, but he didn't stop. He covered himself as thoroughly as he could, even rubbing some into his hair, clothes and pack.

"I freakin' hope this does the trick," he whispered, his voice shaking. He glanced around the forest, his eyes scanning the trees and underbrush. He could hear forest sounds but

couldn't tell if the Sasquatch were watching him or if they were somewhere deeper in the woods. Either way, he couldn't afford to wait.

Levi grabbed his backpack and shoved it into the hollow log first, wedging it tightly into the far end. The bag blocked part of the opening, creating a small barrier between him and the Sasquatch. Taking a deep breath, he slid in after it, feet-first, pulling his knees up to his chest.

The inside was cramped and damp, the bark pressing uncomfortably against his back. He adjusted his position as best he could, making sure his hatchet was within reach. His breathing was shallow, his chest rising and falling with every strained inhale.

He laid his head on his arm, trying to calm himself. His heart was pounding so loudly he was sure it would give him away. "*Just breathe,*" he whispered to himself. "*Just rest for a minute.*"

The log provided a small measure of comfort—at least he was no longer exposed. But the fear clung to him, unrelenting. He knew he wouldn't be truly safe until he escaped this forest. Closing his eyes, he tried to push the nightmare from his mind, but it was futile. Images of Carter, Rob, Tyler and Tyson flashed before him, their faces etched with fear and pain, haunting him with every thought.

Levi's eyes shot open as a new thought hit him like a punch to the gut.

"*Rob...*" he whispered. His mind raced as the pieces fell into place. *Rob had the car keys.*

Panic surged through him, replacing the brief flicker of calm he had found. Without the keys, there was no escape. Even if he made it back to the trailhead, even if he somehow avoided the creatures, he wouldn't be able to leave.

"*Shit,*" Levi mumbled, his voice trembling. He squeezed his eyes shut, his breathing quick and shallow. The log felt smaller now, more suffocating. He couldn't believe he hadn't thought of it sooner.

His chances of survival had plummeted, and the knowledge twisted his gut like a knife. But he forced himself to stay still, to stay quiet. The Sasquatch were still out there, he couldn't risk giving himself away.

"*Stay calm,*" he whispered to himself. "*Just stay calm.*"

Levi forced himself to rest, even if only for a few minutes. He needed to regain his strength—he couldn't afford to stay here long.

For now, though, hiding was his only option.

CHAPTER 30

Levi woke with a sharp gasp, his head jerking upward and hitting the rough inside of the hollow log. Pain shot through his skull, but it was nothing compared to the wave of disorientation that followed. For one fleeting, blissful second, he forgot where he was. Then the reality hit him.

The darkness. The suffocating, damp air. The scratches on his arms and legs from clawing through the overgrown forest.

He was still here. Still in this nightmare.

Levi pressed his back against the rough bark of the log, trying to control his breathing. His limbs screamed in protest as he shifted, cramped from hours in the tight space.

Slowly, he stretched his legs as much as the confined space allowed, the motion sending painful tingles through his muscles. Another discomfort pressed at him—he desperately needed to relieve himself, but fear held him back. The smell of urine could betray his hiding spot, alerting the Sasquatch to where he was. Gritting his teeth, he pushed the urge aside, knowing that even the smallest mistake could be the one that got him killed.

Outside, the forest hummed with life. The chirp of crickets and the rustling of small animals—raccoons or foxes, perhaps—moved through the underbrush, filling the air with a semblance of normalcy.

Levi clung to those sounds. Last night, the forest had gone deathly silent when the Sasquatch were nearby. Now, the return of life gave him a fragile sliver of hope that the creatures were elsewhere—for the moment.

But the memories wouldn't let him breathe. Their reason for entering the forest—friendship, escape, celebration—had vanished, leaving only terror and death in its wake. Levi knew he had to survive, not just for himself but to ensure the truth of what happened to his friends would be known. The thought of their families—or his family—living without answers or closure was unbearable.

And then there was Abby. Her face appeared, unbidden,

as if to taunt him with memories of a life he wasn't sure he'd ever see again. Her laughter, her warm smile—it all felt like another world.

Levi gritted his teeth and pushed the thoughts aside. Dwelling on them, on home, wouldn't help—it would only drag him down. Instead, he let the memories fuel him, igniting a fire within him. He couldn't let his friend's suffering be for nothing. He had to survive, to make it out, and to make sure their stories were told.

Suddenly, he realized the crickets had stopped.

That's when the sound came softly at first, almost blending with the natural hum of the forest. Levi went still, his ears straining to identify the sound.

A faint, high-pitched cry.

The sound was faint, but it made his skin crawl. As he listened, the sound grew louder, more distinct. It was unmistakable now—a baby crying.

Levi's heart pounded in his chest. *A baby? Out here?* The thought surged through his mind, unsettling and impossible to ignore.

The noise rose and fell, the wailing heart-wrenching yet strangely... wrong. The pitch fluctuated unnaturally, just enough to unsettle him. It sounded like a mimic, like someone or something imitating a baby's cries but not quite getting it right.

His stomach twisted as the realization hit him. It wasn't a baby. It was them.

The Sasquatch. Skilled mimics, Levi thought as his blood ran cold.

Were they trying to lure him out? Did they know where he was, hiding in the log? Or were they casting a net, waiting for him to make a mistake?

Don't move. Don't make a sound. Stay calm.

The cries continued, growing louder and more erratic, as if testing his resolve. Levi's muscles screamed from staying in place, but he didn't dare shift. He couldn't reveal his hiding place.

Finally, the crying stopped abruptly.

Levi exhaled shakily, though his heart still pounded. He wasn't sure if the deafening silence was a good sign or a bad one.

A low, rhythmic thudding started, faint at first, but growing louder.

Levi went rigid, every muscle in his body taut. The sound was unmistakable—heavy, deliberate footfalls.

As he listened, he realized something else. There wasn't just one set of footsteps. He could hear three distinct rhythms, each with a slightly different cadence.

Three of them.

Levi's stomach flipped as he strained to focus. The steps were slow and bipedal, moving with an unsettling deliberation. Each thud sent a faint vibration through the log, a grim reminder of their size.

Then came the stench.

A foul, overwhelming odor seeped into the log, a nauseating mix of wet dog, rotting meat, and the acrid punch of skunk. Levi's stomach lurched, and he had to clamp a hand over his mouth to keep from gagging. The smell alone was enough to make him panic, but he managed to stay still. If he gave himself away now, he was as good as dead.

Then came the voices.

They weren't guttural or growling. Instead, the tones shifted wildly—sometimes high-pitched and sharp, like a shriek, other times low, and rumbling, almost musical in their rhythm. It was as though they were speaking a language Levi couldn't even begin to comprehend, their intonations alien and haunting.

The unpredictability of the sounds was the most terrifying part. One voice would rise suddenly, sharp and piercing, only to be met by a low, resonant reply. The effect was both chaotic and calculated, like they were exchanging information in a way humans couldn't understand.

Levi's hands trembled as he listened. The voices carried a strange rhythm, almost hypnotic in their tempo, but every instinct in his body screamed danger.

The footsteps grew louder, closer.

One of the voices released a high-pitched chirp, followed by a deep, resonant tone that seemed to echo through the forest. Levi could feel his pulse in his ears, his heart hammering so loudly he was sure they could hear it.

They were mere feet from the log.

Levi squeezed his eyes shut, willing them to leave. For a horrifying moment, his mind conjured an image of a Sasquatch reaching into the hollow log, its massive hand clamping around his head and yanking him out with brutal force. He fought to suppress the panic that threatened to consume him.

The voices outside rose and fell, the strange language flowing between them. Were they toying with him? Did they already know he was there, cowering in the log?

Minutes stretched into what felt like hours. Then, finally, the footsteps began to move away, fading into the distance.

Levi remained motionless long after the sounds had faded, his body trembling with a mix of fear and exhaustion. Slowly, the forest came back to life, its familiar noises resuming as if nothing had happened.

A shaky breath escaped his lips, and after a minute or two, Levi made himself shift position, his muscles crying out in pain.

"You're going to make it," he whispered to himself, his voice barely audible. "You're getting out of this damn forest."

The creatures were still out there. Levi knew that. But he clung to one thought: *I will survive. I will see Abby again.*

And with that, he settled back into the log, steeling himself for whatever came next.

CHAPTER 31

Levi woke with a sharp, stinging pain on his neck. Instinctively, he slapped at it, only for another sharp bite to jab into his arm. He groaned, swatting at his legs and chest as the burning pain spread. His eyes adjusted to the dim light filtering into the hollow log, and he saw the source—ants. Dozens of them, biting him in relentless waves.

"Shit!" Levi hissed, wriggling out of the log. He tumbled onto the forest floor, brushing frantically at his arms, neck and legs. The ants scattered, but the lingering bites still throbbed like tiny embers on his skin.

As his breathing steadied, the reality of his situation hit him. He was out in the open.

Levi stopped and crouched low as his gaze swept across the forest. His anxiety grew as the familiar dread returned. Were they watching him now?

But all he heard was the hum of insects, and the faint calls of birds. Sunlight streamed through the foliage in golden beams, the forest seeming almost normal.

"It's daylight," Levi whispered to himself, as if saying it aloud made it safer. But the relief was fleeting. He knew the creatures could still be out there. They could be watching right now.

Levi stretched his aching limbs, wincing as his joints protested. His muscles felt like they had been crushed under a heavy weight for hours, every movement stiff and clumsy. He picked up the hatchet and his pack with his dirt-streaked hands and scanned the forest again for any signs of movement.

Nothing stirred. Slowly, he rose to his feet, his body struggling to cooperate with his mind.

He couldn't stay here. He needed to keep moving.

The first few steps were agonizing. His legs felt heavy, his back stiff and unyielding. He pushed through it, forcing himself into a steady rhythm. Each step became a little easier, the stiffness giving way to a dull, throbbing ache.

Twenty minutes into his walk, Levi came to a sudden stop. The ground sloped downward, revealing a sprawling swamp.

Murky water stretched out before him, framed by twisted, crooked trees. The water, still and dark, held a blackness that seemed to absorb every ray of sunlight that dared to touch it.

Levi scanned the swamp, his heart sinking. It stretched as far as he could see, the edges lost in the dense forest.

He weighed his options.

Going around would take hours—maybe even longer—and there was no telling what dangers might lie in the swamp, let alone how cold the water would be. Still, he figured his best chance was to go straight through it.

He stepped closer to the water's edge. The smell hit him first—a foul, earthy stench that clung to the air. Levi grimaced, but he took a deep breath and stepped into the water.

The cold hit him like a slap, the icy chill soaking through his boots instantly. He knew he'd have to move fast to avoid hypothermia.

As he waded forward, the water crept up his legs and

sapped his body heat with every step.

About halfway across, Levi stopped. A loud splash echoed through the swamp, sending ripples across the surface. His breathing becoming even more erratic as his eyes darted to the source.

"Just an animal," he whispered, trying to convince himself. "Probably a muskrat."

As if in response, another splash erupted behind him, this one louder. Levi turned sharply, scanning the water. There was nothing—just the ripples spreading outward, as if something had dipped below the surface.

A heavy thud followed, somewhere to his left. It was the unmistakable sound of something large hitting the ground. Levi's chest tightened.

"Is it following me?" he mumbled to himself.

Another thud came, closer this time. Levi's instincts screamed at him to move. He picked up his pace, his breaths coming faster as the cold water rose to his waist.

The swamp seemed to grow darker as he pressed on, the canopy above thickening and blocking out the light. Levi was swimming now, the water too deep to walk through. His clothes clung to him like a second skin, heavy and restricting.

Then his foot caught on something beneath the surface.

Levi fought to keep calm, his body tensing as he fought to free himself. His pants were caught on a submerged branch, anchoring him in place.

A wave of panic surged as he pulled harder, but the branch held firm, refusing to let go.

"*Come on,*" he whispered through gritted teeth. He twisted and pulled with all his strength, the water around him churning violently.

The splashes from earlier echoed in his mind, and Levi's panic escalated. His breathing quickened as he clawed at the branch. Finally, with a loud rip, his pants tore free, sending him stumbling forward.

With a heart pounding rush, he plunged back into the water, as his gaze swept across the swamp. It was quiet again—too quiet.

Ignoring it, Levi pushed forward, each step and stroke a battle against his aching limbs and the icy cold water. His body screamed for rest, but he refused to stop.

Finally, after what seemed like an endless struggle, the

water began to recede. Levi staggered onto dry land, collapsing onto the ground. He gasped for air, his body trembling violently from exhaustion and the icy cold that had seeped into his bones.

His soaked jacket hung heavily on him, offering no warmth. With shaking hands, he peeled it off and tossed it aside—it was useless now. Shivering uncontrollably, he rubbed his arms and legs, desperate to generate some heat. It was a small comfort against the relentless chill that clung to him as if it were a second skin.

For a moment, he lay there, staring up at the canopy above. The swamp stretched out like a dark, malevolent presence, but he was through it. He had made it.

Levi forced himself to sit up, grabbing his hatchet and pack. He couldn't afford to linger. The forest around him remained vast and unforgiving, and he had to get his muscles moving again.

He rose unsteadily, his legs shaking beneath him as he took a tentative step forward. His teeth chattered as he whispered, *"Keep going. Just keep going."*

And with that, he continued onward into the unknown.

CHAPTER 32

After an hour of trudging through the forest, Levi couldn't tell if the dampness clinging to him was from the swamp or his own sweat. Either way, it didn't matter. All that mattered was getting out of this nightmare, and the only way to do that was to keep moving forward.

He knew he was lost. The trail had vanished, whether yesterday or this morning, he wasn't sure. What concerned him more was the nagging fear that he was heading in the wrong direction. If that was the case, he could only hope to stumble across a road or a house—anything that offered even the faintest chance of safety.

Levi pushed through the brush, swiping branches out of his way, when he felt it. The air around him grew heavier, colder, and charged with a suffocating weight. His senses recognized it immediately. His hands trembled as he gripped the hatchet tighter, every instinct screaming at him to run.

Then the first whoops shattered the uneasy quiet.

They were back.

Levi's stomach dropped. That same voice from yesterday roared in his head, urgent and unrelenting: *Move!*

He broke into a sprint, his legs pounding the forest floor as fast as they could carry him. The whooping sounds grew louder, more erratic, echoing through the trees like a primal siren. He knew he couldn't outrun them forever, but he sure as hell was going to try.

He dodged trees and vaulted over roots, his lungs burning with every breath, his heart hammering in his chest. The forest felt endless, the dense canopy overhead blotting out the weak morning light. Every crashing noise behind him pushed him harder, the pounding footsteps of his pursuers drawing closer.

Then, slicing through the cacophony of whoops and snapping branches, he heard something else. A faint, rhythmic whooshing sound, distant but steady. Levi's ears strained to identify it, his hope flickering like a match.

A helicopter.

"Oh, please let them see me," he said, his eyes darting frantically, searching for the source of the sound.

To his right, the dense canopy began to thin, sunlight breaking through small gaps in the trees. Levi veered sharply toward it, desperation fueling his aching legs. The crashing sounds of his pursuers grew louder, but he pushed onward, his breath ragged.

Finally, he burst through the thinning tree line and into a field. His heart skipped a beat at the sight. It was wide and open, bathed in the golden glow of the rising sun, with tall grass swaying gently in the breeze. This was it—his salvation. Out here, the helicopter would see him. Out here, he had a chance.

Tilting his head upward, he scanned the sky, and then he saw it—a helicopter. Its blades cut through the air, the sound growing louder with every second.

Levi waved one arm frantically as he kept running, his other hand clutching the hatchet in a death grip. *"Please see me,"* he begged, his voice hoarse. *"Please."*

The crashing in the trees behind him grew deafening, branches snapping like gunshots. Levi didn't look back. He couldn't. If he stopped now, even briefly, he knew he'd be dead.

The field stretched out endlessly before him, but the helicopter's roar gave him hope. This was his only chance—and he wasn't going to let it slip away.

CHAPTER 33

The roar of the helicopter blades filled the air, their steady rhythm pulsing through Levi's chest as he sprinted across the open field. Every step was a battle against exhaustion, his legs screaming in protest and his lungs burning from the cold morning air.

The helicopter hovered low, its dark silhouette stark against the pale sky. The side door slid open, and a man leaned out, scanning the field. Suddenly, his body stiffened, his wide-eyed shock unmistakable.

"Oh my God," the man said quietly before shouting at Levi with desperate urgency. "Move! They're coming!"

Out of the tree line burst a massive Sasquatch, running upright on two legs as it led the charge. Its muscular frame moved with terrifying speed, each stride powerful and unyielding. Behind it, two others bounded on all fours, their swift, and predatory strides eating up the ground. Their guttural screams carried over the sound of the rotors, chilling Levi to the core.

Levi's stomach dropped, but he didn't look back. He didn't need to. The man's panicked tone told him everything—they were close. Too close.

"Hurry!" the man yelled, his voice rising with panic as he waved frantically.

Inside the cockpit, the front passenger craned his neck to see what the commotion was about. When his eyes locked on the creatures, his jaw dropped. "What in God's name are those?!" he barked.

"What's going on?" the pilot snapped, glancing to his side.

They're coming out of the woods!" the passenger shouted. "Big… huge… hell… I don't know what the heck they are! You're gonna have to take off damn fast, Ace," he yelled into the mouthpiece.

Ace squinted, his grip tightening on the controls as he peered out the side window. His mouth fell open, and a string of curses tumbled out as he finally saw them.

Levi reached the helicopter just as his legs threatened to give out. The man at the door grabbed his arm and yanked him upward with all his strength.

"Get in!" the man shouted, pulling him inside.

Levi scrambled into the cabin, collapsing onto the floor in a heap. His breath came in short, painful gasps as he yelled, "Go! Take off! Now!"

The man slammed the door shut with a resounding thud, locking them inside just as the helicopter began to lift.

"Get us outta here dammit!!" the man shouted, twisting to look out the window.

The helicopter lurched violently upward as the pilot yanked the controls, the sudden motion slamming Levi into the back of a seat. Pain shot through his shoulder as his head thudded against the frame.

"Jesus!" the passenger shouted, gripping the dashboard as his stomach did cartwheels.

"Hold on!" the pilot yelled, pulling the helicopter into a steep climb. The sharp ascent sent a jolt through everyone, pressing their bodies against their restraints or, in Levi's case, the floor.

Through the small window, Levi caught a glimpse of the largest Sasquatch. It leapt into the air, its massive arms reaching toward the helicopter. For a horrifying moment, he thought it might reach them.

But the creature fell short, crashing back down with enough force to shake the earth. The two on all fours skidded to a stop, their heads snapping upward to watch the helicopter rise. Their frustrated screams faded into the distance as the helicopter climbed higher, leaving them behind.

"Holy shit that was close," the man near the door said, slumping in his seat as he stared at Levi. "What in God's name were those things?"

Levi didn't answer. He couldn't. His chest heaved, each breath a struggle as his body trembled from exhaustion and adrenaline.

The passenger leaned back against the seat, his hands gripping the armrests tightly. "I can't believe what I just saw, Hell, I have no idea what I just saw." he said, shaking his head.

Levi lay on the floor, staring blankly at the ceiling of the small cabin. Every muscle in his body ached, and his thoughts swirled in chaotic fragments, struggling to comprehend what just happened.

I made it, he thought, the realization hitting him like a wave.

For the first time in what felt like forever, Levi allowed himself to believe he might actually survive this nightmare.

CHAPTER 34

The helicopter settled into a steady rhythm after its violent take off, the hum of the blades filling the cabin. Levi lay on the floor, his body trembling from exhaustion and adrenaline. Each breath was quick and uneven, burning inside him. Every muscle ached, his limbs heavy and sluggish, but he was alive.

A wave of nausea hit him suddenly. Levi pressed a hand to his mouth, his other hand loosening its grip on the hatchet until it clattered to the floor. He motioned weakly to his stomach. The older man kneeling beside him caught on immediately and reached behind him, pulling a brown paper bag from a side compartment.

"Here," the man said, handing it over.

Levi snatched the bag and retched into it, his body convulsing with the effort. Mostly liquid splattered into the bottom, the acidic tang burning his throat and stinging his nostrils. When the heaving finally stopped, he slumped back against the wall, the bag still clenched in his trembling hands.

"Hey, kid," the man said, his voice cutting through the hum of the rotors. He leaned closer, concern etched into his weathered face. Reaching behind him, he grabbed a spare headset and slid it over Levi's head.

"This'll make it easier for us to hear each other over the noise," the man said, adjusting the straps and tapping the microphone. "You with me?"

Levi nodded weakly, his voice still caught in his throat as he attempted to steady his breathing.

"I'm Mike," the man said, his voice crackling through the intercom. "That's Larry up front in the passenger seat, and Ace is flying this thing. What's your name?"

"Levi," he rasped, his voice strained.

Mike nodded and glanced down, noticing the hatchet lying on the floor. He picked it up carefully, giving Levi a quick, assessing look, then tucked it securely into a nearby storage pocket.

"Drink this. You look like you need it," Mike said, pulling a bottle of water from a nearby compartment and handing it to Levi.

Levi took the bottle with trembling hands, twisting off the cap. He drank greedily, the cool water soothing his raw throat and washing away the dryness. "Thanks," he croaked.

"Here," Mike said, reaching behind him again. This time, he pulled out a folded blanket and draped it gently over Levi's shoulders. "You're looking pretty beat up, kid. Can't say you smell so good either."

Larry, the man in the front seat, turned slightly to glance at Levi. "Mike's right. You look like you've been through hell."

Levi forced a shaky nod, his throat tightening with emotion. "I... thank you. All of you. If you hadn't been there... I don't think I'd be here right now."

Ace's voice broke through the intercom. "Damn right you wouldn't. But you've got some explaining to do, Levi. What the hell were you running from?"

Levi hesitated, staring at the floor of the cabin. His mind churned as he tried to put the nightmare into words. Finally, he swallowed hard and began to speak.

"They... they killed my friends," he said, his voice uneven.

"We were camping… and I'm the only one still alive."

Mike's eyes widened. "Holy crap. I'm so sorry about your friends," he said sincerely.

Larry swiveled slightly in his seat. "Were they Bigfoot? I mean, that's what they looked like, right? Ugliest damn things I've ever seen."

Levi gripped the water bottle tightly, as he nodded. His voice was low, almost a whisper. "They're evil."

Mike exhaled slowly, exchanging a glance with Larry before turning back to Levi. "Well, kid, whatever those things were, you've got to be the luckiest guy on the planet."

"I know, and I can't thank you guys enough for saving me," Levi said. "I still can't believe I made it."

Larry leaned forward, tapping the map clipped to the dashboard. "If the Bigfoot didn't get you and you kept going in the direction you were heading, you'd have had twenty miles of dense forest ahead of you. No trails, no help, just endless wilderness. No way anyone would've found you."

Levi blinked, the gravity of Larry's words sinking in. "Holy shit," he whispered. "I guess I got turned around. I just… I kept running and running, and it felt like they wouldn't let me leave."

He hesitated, glancing between the men before continuing, his voice quieter. "Can I ask why you were even out here?"

"We're with the DNR," Mike explained. "We were out tracking a wolf pack that's been moving through the area. We use the helicopter to follow their movements across the terrain."

Larry chuckled lightly, his tone softening. "Yeah, and then Mike here spotted you out of the corner of his eye. Thought you were a deer at first."

Mike shook his head. "We didn't realize you were a person until we got a little closer. You're damn lucky we were flying low enough to spot you. We'd only been in the air about eight minutes before we picked you up."

Levi managed a faint smile. "I'm so grateful. Really."

The cabin grew quiet, the hum of the rotors filling the void.

Ace spoke up, his tone thoughtful. "You know, I've been with the DNR for thirty years, and I've never seen a Bigfoot."

Levi looked up at him, his expression grim. "That doesn't mean they didn't see you."

Ace's shoulders stiffened, and a deep crease formed between his brows as the reality sank in. For the first time, he considered the unsettling possibility that Levi was right—those creatures had been out there all along, watching, unseen.

Larry let out a breath, shaking his head. "I still can't process what I saw. You're one strong bastard for keeping it together, son. You know that?"

"I guess I had no choice," Levi said quietly.

Mike shook his head. "What we saw... that was something else. The way they moved, the way they worked together—it was like they were hunting him."

"They were," Levi confirmed, his voice a mere whisper.

The men exchanged uneasy glances, the thought settling over them like a dark cloud.

Larry cleared his throat. "You sure your friends are gone? I mean, do we need to contact law enforcement urgently?"

Levi nodded grimly. "Yeah. They're gone. I saw it happen."

Ace spoke up, his tone steady. "Don't worry, Levi. We're on our way to Duluth. You'll get checked out at the hospital and meet with law enforcement there.”

“Thank you,” Levi said softly.

He stared out the window, his eyes focused on the endless expanse of trees stretching to the horizon. From up here, the forest looked peaceful, its canopy painted with shades of orange and gold from the autumn leaves. But Levi knew better. He knew what was hiding in those shadows.

“You’re safe now, kid,” Mike said as he patted him on the shoulder gently.

Levi nodded faintly, the words echoing in his mind. *Safe.* The three men couldn’t possibly understand just how much those words meant.

EPILOGUE

Rob jolted awake, his heart pounding as if shocked back to life. His eyes darted around in panic, struggling to piece together where he was. The last thing he remembered was the massive hand of the Sasquatch grabbing him, lifting him like a child's toy, and the blur of trees rushing past as he was carried through the forest. In those frantic moments, he had caught a fleeting glimpse of Levi, standing frozen in horror, powerless to do anything but watch as he was taken. That image had seared itself into Rob's mind, a cruel reminder of just how helpless he was.

Now, he was on the ground, surrounded by them.

The clearing was unlike anything he'd seen before—a secluded sanctuary deep in the forest, walled in by towering cliffs on three sides. The mouth of a dark cave yawned open in one corner, its shadow stretching out like a sinister warning. Around him, dozens of Sasquatch loomed, their massive forms blocking out what little light filtered through the canopy above.

The stench hit him first. It was overwhelming—an unbearable mixture of wet dog, rotting vegetation, and something sharp, like ammonia, that he couldn't place. The smell wrapped around him, suffocating and thick. Rob gagged violently, doubling over as his stomach twisted. He tried to hold it in, but it was no use. He retched, his body convulsing as he vomited onto the forest floor.

A low, guttural growl came from one of the Sasquatch nearby, its eyes locking onto him with a menacing glare. Rob wiped his mouth with the back of his hand, his breath stuttering as the creature stepped closer. Its lips curled back, revealing jagged, yellowed teeth, and a rumble reverberated from its massive chest—a warning.

Around him, the other Sasquatch reacted, some tilting their heads curiously while others snarled, their eyes narrowing.

The air crackled with tension, their guttural sounds rising and falling in a strange rhythm that felt like a language all its own.

The creatures were communicating.

Rob thought he'd been terrified when he was taken, but this was something else entirely. His body locked up, every muscle refusing to respond as a hot, humiliating wetness spread down his leg. He barely registered it, his mind consumed by pure panic.

The same Sasquatch that had growled sniffed the air, its nostrils flaring. Its eyes narrowed, and it released another deep, guttural growl—this one harsher, more intense. Rob flinched, his breath quickening as the creature leaned closer, its teeth bared in what could only be described as disgust.

Rob's breathing was quick and shallow as he lowered his gaze and frantically prayed quietly.

Strange guttural sounds filled the air as they grunted, growled, and barked at one another. Their gestures were wild and exaggerated, their massive hands swinging as they pointed at him, the cave, and the forest beyond.

One Sasquatch stood apart from the rest, immediately catching Rob's attention. It was larger, its fur streaked with gray, and its face had a strikingly human quality—intelligent and weathered, as though it had seen decades of life. This one had an aura of authority, its movements thoughtful and commanding.

The leader bellowed, its booming growls cutting through the chaos. It pointed at Rob, then gestured sharply toward the forest, roaring with an intensity that made Rob's stomach twist.

The others responded with a frenzy of sounds—snarls, growls, and sharp barks filled the clearing. Some creatures stomped their feet and swiped at the air, their agitation clear. Rob had no idea what they were arguing about, but their divided reactions made one thing obvious: he was the center of their dispute.

Rob's senses began to take in more of his surroundings, though his body remained paralyzed with fear.

He noticed smaller Sasquatch—juveniles, he guessed— peeking out from behind larger ones, their wide, curious eyes fixed on him. They were smaller but no less intimidating, their movements quick and jerky as they observed him from what they clearly thought was a safe distance.

Rob shifted slightly, trying to sit up straighter, but the smallest movement drew low snarls from a few of the Sasquatch. One, standing to his left, stepped closer, hissing at him. Rob lowered his gaze, his heart hammering in his chest.

Looking past the creatures, his eyes fixed on the distant

edge of the clearing. A sudden storm of emotions crashed over him—anger, sadness, and dread.

There, arranged like a gruesome warning, were the bodies of his friends—and two others he didn't recognize.

Tyler's body was slumped against a jagged branch stuck in the ground, the left side of his face caved in, his features barely recognizable. His lifeless eyes stared into the distance, frozen in his final moment of terror.

Tyson was sprawled unnaturally on the ground nearby, his head twisted sharply to one side. His neck had been snapped clean, the jagged angle of his head enough to send a wave of nausea through Rob.

Above them, Carter's body hung impaled on a massive tree branch, the wood skewering him just below the ribs. His neck was also broken, his head tilted at an unnatural angle, his limbs dangling limply as though mocking the idea of life. The faint sway of his body in the breeze added to the grotesque display, making it seem like a deliberate, calculated arrangement.

Nearby, two other bodies lay crumpled in the dirt. Rob couldn't make out their injuries, but the lifeless way they were sprawled told him enough. He didn't know who they were, but their presence made one thing clear: the Sasquatch didn't stop with his friends.

Rob's stomach twisted, bile rising in his throat as the stench of death mixed with the reek of the Sasquatch. He clamped his mouth shut, swallowing hard to keep himself from retching again.

This wasn't just death. It was a message.

Rob's vision blurred as he forced himself to look away, his hands curling into fists in a desperate attempt to steady them. Tears streaked down his cheeks.

Then another thought struck him, cutting through the haze of horror. He hadn't seen Levi's body among the others. For the first time, a faint flicker of hope stirred inside him. Maybe he made it out. Maybe Levi escaped.

The leader's roar snapped Rob back to the Sasquatches. Its sharp, piercing gaze locked onto Rob, and for a second, Rob wondered if it was considering what to do with him—or if it already had a plan.

Rob could sense the tension escalating with every growl and movement. The creatures were divided—some seemed to side with the leader, their postures calm but watchful, while others stomped and roared, their hostility directed not just at him but at a few of the Sasquatches he assumed were responsible for bringing him here. The air was thick with unspoken conflict, each guttural sound and aggressive gesture adding to the charged atmosphere.

They're arguing about me, Rob thought. But why? Did they bring me here by mistake? Or was I brought here for a reason?

His mind raced through possibilities, each one more horrifying than the last. Were they deciding whether to kill him? Eat him? Or was he some kind of bargaining chip for whatever these creatures valued?

One of the Sasquatch stomped toward the leader, its deep growl carrying an air of defiance. It gestured aggressively toward Rob, slamming its massive hand into the ground for emphasis. The leader responded with a thunderous roar, its tone sharp and imposing.

The intensity of their exchange made Rob's stomach flip. The group seemed on the verge of turning violent, and he was caught in the middle of it.

The leader barked one final, deafening command, silencing the others. Its sharp, piercing gaze scanned the group before it gestured dismissively toward Rob. The others hesitated but eventually backed off, their snarls fading into low growls as they retreated slightly.

Rob stayed perfectly still, his breath shallow as he tried to process what had just happened. The leader turned away, moving toward the cave, and the rest of the group began to disperse, though a few continued to cast wary, hostile glances in his direction.

Whatever decision had been made, Rob didn't know.

Left alone in the clearing, Rob's terror didn't subside—it only deepened. He had no idea what the creatures planned to do with him, but he knew he couldn't stay here.

His gaze drifted toward the cliffs and the dense forest behind him. There had to be a way out, but every scenario that crossed his mind ended with him being caught—and likely killed.

They won't decide my fate, he thought, his fists clenching. They're formidable, even intelligent—but I'm more intelligent. I'll outthink them, outsmart them, and find a way out of this nightmare.

ABOUT THE AUTHOR

 Luka T. Jacobs, an author from the picturesque Illawarra region south of Sydney, Australia, is passionate about cryptids like Sasquatch and Dogman. She lives there with her partner and their dog, Finnigan.

Luka's love for animals and adventure fuels her storytelling. With a background in Graphic Design and Art, she adds a unique visual flair to her work. An avid traveler and explorer, she draws inspiration from the wild, eager to share her imaginative worlds with readers.

Luka T. Jacobs

Stay connected and join the conversation!

FB: https://www.facebook.com/lukatjacobs

A: https://amazon.com/author/lukatjacobs

W: http://www.LukaTJacobs.com

JOIN CRYPTID HORROR CENTRAL

Join my email list and get first access to new releases and download my **FREE** short story *"The Dogman of Coldwater Creek"*.

WWW.LUKATJACOBS.COM

Dear Reader,

Thank you for diving into my book amidst a sea of choices—it truly means the world to me.

If you enjoyed the story, I'd love it if you shared your experience with others and left a review. As an independent author, your voice helps bring these tales to life for more readers, and every recommendation makes a tremendous impact.

Thank you again for joining me on this journey. I'm so grateful to have you as a reader!

SNEAK PEAK:
SAVAGE ROGUE:
A NICOLE BERETTI THRILLER

Crack.

A sharp snap echoed through the dense Wyoming underbrush, but Tucker and Bo barely registered it as they trudged forward, their boots sinking into the damp forest floor. Shotguns hung from their shoulders, swinging slightly with each step as they moved in tandem. The sun's first light crept slowly over the horizon, slicing through the thick morning fog that clung low to the ground, casting an eerie glow over the wilderness.

Both men, rugged and in their early thirties, were marked by a long history of poor decisions and run-ins with the law. This morning was no different. They'd spent months running an illegal trapping operation, specifically targeting grizzly bears for their lucrative pelts. Their greed dulled any caution they might have felt about their scheme's dangers.

The payday was all that mattered—enough to keep them going, no matter the risk or the rules they had to break.

"Man, I'm telling ya, this is it. If we succeed in trapping another grizzly, we'll be all set for the whole winter," Bo exclaimed, his voice hoarse from years of tobacco addiction. He hocked a loogie onto the dirt and fixed his grimy baseball hat.

"It better be worth it, that's all I'm saying. Ain't no way I'm freezin' my ass off for nothin'," Tucker grumbled, pulling his jacket tighter against the cold. He was thinner and shorter than Bo, his eyes darting nervously around the forest, always on the lookout. He knew they'd be in trouble if the game wardens caught them.

A few days ago, they set up a large bear trap hidden in the forest. Made of heavy-duty steel, the contraption was designed to trap anything that ventured onto the game trails. Bo purchased it from a dubious out-of-state source, boasting that no creature could escape once its jaws closed.

"Damn thing's strong enough to catch a tank," Bo had said when they set it. "Ain't no bear getting outta this one."

The trap had been carefully set along a narrow game trail, hidden just off a small clearing where animals often ventured through. They'd chosen the location to catch an unsuspecting grizzly on its routine path, banking on the season's chill to drive it along established trails. The payout for a full bear hide, they figured, would be worth all the freezing mornings—and the constant fear of getting nabbed by Fish and Game wardens.

Tucker kicked at a patch of dirt as they neared the clearing where the trap was set. "Think we got one?"

"If we did, it ain't goin' nowhere. This trap'll hold," Bo said, slapping Tucker on the back.

As they entered the clearing, both men suddenly stopped. Something big was caught in the trap.

"What the hell...?" Tucker said, squinting through the misty dawn light.

A huge creature, bigger than any bear they had ever witnessed, lay partially slouched on the forest ground. At first glance, they thought it might be a wolf, but as their eyes adjusted, it was clear this was no ordinary wolf. The creature was massive, measuring well over six feet in length, covered in thick, tangled fur, and possessed a formidable physique that resembled a creature from a nightmare rather than a real animal.

Its leg was ensnared in the steel jaws of the bear trap, the metal teeth piercing flesh and fur. The ground around the trap was covered in blood, dark and sticky in the faint light, and the soil indicated a struggle had occurred. The beast had clearly fought to free itself. The area around the trap was churned up, deep claw imprints etched into the earth where the creature had thrashed and tried to escape.

"Holy hell..." Bo whispered, stepping forward cautiously. "We... we got somethin' big. The boss is gonna love it!"

Tucker's stomach churned at the sight. "I-Is it... is it d-dead?"

Bo grinned. "Sure looks like it.

"Look at the trap," Tucker said, his voice trembling slightly. "Thing put up one hell of a fight."

Bo chuckled and approached the creature without hesitation. "Thing's as good as dead. Hell, it ain't movin' at all." He stood right next to its side, eyes gleaming with greed, and gave it a sharp kick to the ribs.

Tucker squinted, feeling a pit form in his stomach as he took in the massive, slumped form on the ground. "What... what the hell is that?"

Bo chuckled and stepped forward without hesitation. "This, my friend, is one huge freakin' wolf. The boss is gonna pay us big-time for this." His eyes lit up as he admired the creature's massive limbs and thick fur. "I woke up with a good feeling about today."

Tucker hesitated, casting a wary glance left and right, his nerves prickling as he took in the creature's massive form. "That... that ain't a normal wolf, Bo. It's too big. Looks like a freakin' werewolf or somethin'." His voice dropped to a whisper. "Maybe we should just leave it. Somethin' about this don't feel right, I tell ya."

Bo laughed, brushing off Tucker's concern. "What are you scared of, Tuck? This thing's our payday, and it's not even breathin'." He nudged the creature's side with his boot, his grin widening. "It's dead, see?"

Tucker's gut twisted, but he stayed silent, glancing around the clearing. The thick mist clung to the air, as the hairs on his neck bristled. "Alright... let's make it quick," he said, looking away from the creature's enormous form.

Bo knelt down beside the trap, his fingers fumbling with the latch. "Tucker, give me a hand with this," he said. Together, they pried the trap open, and with a metallic click, the jaws sprang apart, freeing the creature's leg.

For a moment, silence hung heavy in the air.

Then, in a sudden, terrifying blur, something exploded from the shadows—a dark, hulking figure hurtling out of the trees with the speed and force of a freight train. Tucker barely registered what was happening before the creature was upon them, claws flashing in the dim light.

Bo's scream was short-lived as the creature's claws tore through his side, ripping through muscle and bone with ease. Blood sprayed across the clearing, splattering Tucker's face as he stumbled back, frozen in horror. Bo's eyes widened in shock, his hands clutching at the gaping wound in his chest as he staggered, his mouth opening in a silent scream.

The creature didn't hesitate. It lunged at Bo, driving him to the ground with bone-crushing force, its jaws closing around his throat. With a sickening crunch, its teeth tore through flesh, tendons and muscle, severing his spinal column in a single, brutal motion. Blood pooled beneath him, soaking into the dirt as his body went still, his lifeless eyes staring at the misty sky above.

"Oh, God... oh, Jesus Christ!" Tucker stammered, his body shaking as he stumbled backward, his gaze locked on the creature that now turned its attention toward him.

The beast loomed, massive and unnatural, its muzzle dripping with blood. beneath its dense fur as it stood there, staring down at Bo's mangled body with eyes that burned with a terrifying, almost human rage.

Tucker stared, transfixed, as it rose slowly onto two legs, towering over him, its broad shoulders heaving with every breath. The creature's eyes locked onto him, sharp and intelligent, gleaming with a hunger that turned his blood to ice.

Tucker felt the scream clawing its way up his throat, his mind urging him to run, but his legs were leaden, frozen by terror. The shotgun strapped across his shoulder was all but forgotten, dead weight in the haze of fear clouding his mind.

Then, with a low, guttural growl that reverberated in his chest, the beast lunged, closing the distance in a heartbeat. Its jaws clamped down on his arm, bone crunching beneath the brutal force, and in a single, terrifying wrench, it tore his arm clean off. A white-hot pain exploded through him as his scream shattered the morning silence, echoing through the trees while blood sprayed from the wound, staining the earth.

Tucker staggered backward, clutching at the raw, bleeding stump, his vision blurring as his strength ebbed with every heartbeat. His breaths came in shallow, panicked gasps as he stumbled through the underbrush, leaving a crimson trail in his wake.

But the beast wasn't finished.

With frightening speed, it lunged again, slashing at his legs with its powerful claws. Tucker crashed to the ground, his body convulsing in agony as blood poured from the gashes. His vision darkened at the edges, the world spinning as he struggled to breathe, his strength fading.

The creature stood over him, its gaze unwavering as it watched his life ebb away. Tucker's last, desperate attempt to crawl away was met with a swift, brutal bite, severing his leg in one savage twist. The pain was blinding, his mind barely able to comprehend the extent of his injuries as he lay helpless, his blood seeping into the earth.

With one final, ragged breath, Tucker went still, his body slumping in the grass as the life drained from him.

The creature remained for a moment, breathing heavily, its body tense as it surveyed the bloody remains of the two humans who had caused his sister's death. For a brief moment, its gaze softened as it turned back toward the lifeless form of its sibling, lying still and broken on the forest floor.

As the creature drew near, it moved with a haunting grace, dropping to all fours and lowering its massive head to nuzzle her gently, emitting a soft, mournful whine. It lingered beside her, its fury momentarily softened by a sorrow that settled deep within its chest.

Then, with one last, lingering look at the clearing, it turned and melted back into the woods, disappearing into the dense underbrush. The mist closed around it, swallowing its form as it silently left the clearing behind.

Twists you won't see coming. Suspense you'll never forget. _Savage Rogue_ is here—download for FREE with Kindle Unlimited!

The hairs on the back of your neck will never lay flat again.

CURRENT TITLES

AS AT NOV. 24